On the Edges of Elfland

On the Edges of Elfland

A Fairy-Tale for Grown Ups

DAVID RUSSELL MOSLEY

RESOURCE *Publications* · Eugene, Oregon

ON THE EDGES OF ELFLAND
A Fairy-Tale for Grown Ups

Resource Publications
An Imprint of Wipf and Stock Publishers
199 W. 8th Ave., Suite 3
Eugene, OR 97401

www.wipfandstock.com

PAPERBACK ISBN: 978-1-4982-7933-8
HARDCOVER ISBN: 978-1-4982-7935-2
EBOOK ISBN: 978-1-4982-7934-5

Manufactured in the U.S.A.   10/04/16

To the men and women of the British Faërie Tradition,
May I have written a work that you would have wanted to read.

And I serve the fairy queen.

—William Shakespeare,
A Midsummer Night's Dream Act I, Scene I.

Preface

This book began nearly ten years ago as a project for a class taught by my friend, Cliff Wheeler. Now it has evolved and hopefully matured. Along with thanking those who have made this book possible, I want to take a brief moment to explain this book's substitle. I have called this book *A Fairy-Tale for Grown-Ups*, borrowing, in part, the oft forgotten subtitle to C.S. Lewis' *That Hideous Strength*. We have come to a point, really this began at least during the Victorian Era, where fairy-tales are considered to be stories for children. While someone like J.R.R. Tolkien would rightfully explain to us that this is untrue of the traditional fairy-tale, it is certainly what the Disneyfication of so many tradiational tales have come to be. This story, therefore, is a fairy-tale for grown-ups, for people who used to read fairy-tales as children but have since stopped; for people who never picked up a fairy-tale thinking them childish fantasies. This is a fairy-tale for grown-ups and that does not mean it is full of sex or ambiguity. Rather, I hope, it is a reminder of the truths that fairy-tales can teach us when we listen. In any event, I simply hope you think it a good story and one worth reading.

David Russell Mosley
The Feast of St. Mary Magdalen, 2016

Acknowledgements

There are so many people to thank for the publication of this book. I must, of course, first thank my friend, Cliff Wheeler, for being the first reader of the early versions of this story. I also thank the small group of writers that met not long after I first began this story who heard early chapters and commented on them. Without the encouragement of Caryn Collins, my wife's former Head Resident in college, I do not think I would have attempted to finish this book the first time around. I also thank those who read later versions of the story both in private and online who gave me hope that this was a story worth reading. To my parents, who always encouraged their strange son's strange writing, I too must say thank you. I must also thank my wife who supported me starting this story over again when I was in the second year of my PhD. I thank also my children who helped inspire me to publish this book so I could have something to pass on to them. I also thank God Almighty, the Poet who inspires us, who desires us to imitate him as sub-creators for whatever gifts I have with the proverbial pen.

Chapter 1

In the village of Carlisle, which is located in the depths of modern England, near the summit of the mountain Dweormount, and surrounded by a wood called Fey Forest there was born a boy called Alfred Perkins. There was nothing particularly remarkable about Alfred's birth. He was born on 25 March with no pomp or circumstance. There were no shining stars in the sky that day that ought not to have been there. Nothing particularly special happened in the village to signify the birth of this boy. No, he was born like any other child.

His parents' named him Alfred after stories an old man in the village told. They loved this old man, a certain Mr. Oliver Cyning, and made him Alfred's godfather at his christening. The priest who presided over the christening was an elderly man, a certain Fr. Nicholas. He was aided by his curate, Fr. Stratford. Fr. Nicholas, bathed the boy Alfred and blessed him. Alfred's parents then held a celebration at their home.

The Perkinses were the landlords of an old fashioned style inn, which was well known for the quality of its beer and the scrumptiousness of its food. The Broken Spoke, for so the inn was named, did not have any of those trendy things one finds in pubs throughout the rest of England, or that can be found in nearly every bar in America. It lacked televisions, gambling machines, and loud music (unless it was one of the local bands who played there on occasion). The layout was more like a mismatched home than a restaurant and that is just how George and Jessica, Alfred's parents, liked it.

Most nights, if you were to enter The Broken Spoke, you would likely hear Mr. Cyning telling one of his stories. They were typically stories of the fantastical and dealt with local myths and legends. As Alfred grew into boyhood, he came to love these stories. Most days would either find him sitting in the pub listening to Mr. Cyning or running about in Fey Forest pretending he was having his own adventures.

Typically when he returned from these jaunts he would make his parents and godfather sit down and listen to his stories. One day, when Alfred was about ten years old he came home with a rather different story. He gathered his parents and godfather into one of the rooms of the pub and began: "You'll never guess what I saw today."

"A bird," said his mother.

"A deer," said his father.

"A mushroom," said his godfather, "as big as your head."

"Nope," he replied, looking pleased that they had not guessed. "You'll never guess."

"Well then, tell us, Alfie," his mother replied.

"Today, I saw a fairy or maybe it was a pixie. I don't know the difference yet, but I saw one all the same. It was taking care of some wild flowers in the forest. It had tiny little wings and very long arms."

"Did it, now?" his father said with a grin.

"What did it say, Alfie?" asked his mother. His godfather sat in silence.

"Why it didn't say anything, Mum. It just went about its business until it noticed me and then flew away fast. I tried to follow it, but it went up, up into the trees where I could not follow." He said this with a hint of sadness.

"Don't fret, my boy," said his father clapping him on the back. "I'm sure there will be more opportunities for you to hunt fairies in the forest."

"Oh no, Father. I would never hunt them, I only want to watch them and learn what they do."

"Quite right," chimed in his godfather. "It wouldn't do to go hunting fairies, you never know what might happen. They can be mighty mischievous. Why I know one story about a group of brownies who had something to say about the name and running of this inn."

"I've never heard that one. Do tell it, Mr. Cyning," said Alfred excitedly. His parents smiled, having heard the story many times before themselves.

Mr. Cyning, sat up straight and began the story, "The Broken Spoke had just been finished. It was not, however, called The Broken Spoke to begin with. Originally, it was called The Tarnished Bell. It was called Tarnished Bell because the tavern owner Henry Bucklin, great grandfather of the Mr. Bucklin who sold The Broken Spoke to Thomas Brandy nearly thirty-five years ago now, has it really been that long. . . Where was I?"

"It was named The Tarnished Bell because Henry Bucklin—"

"—Because Henry Bucklin used an old, lacklustre bell to let people know when the tavern was open. He hadn't quite set on a name until he heard two of his patrons out and about in town say, 'Oi, are you going to the tarnished bell this evening?'

"'You know I am, Wilfred, we go there every evening and enjoy a few pints. I tell you, I don't know what I'd do if it weren't for the tarnished bell. I sometimes think I live to hear it ring in the evenings, work bein' what it is and all. Well, I see you there after work Wilfred.'

"'Right then, I'll see you tonight, Franklin.'

"'The Tarnished Bell,' thought old Henry Bucklin to himself, 'that isn't a bad name for my tavern, not a bad name at all.' So the next day Henry set about making the sign. He worked well into the evening to the point where he fell asleep with the sign unfinished.

"Now, there happened to be a group of brownies that lived near the tavern."

"What exactly are brownies?" asked Alfred.

"Brownies are small creatures, not more than six inches high, most of them. They've got little mouse like tales and long whiskers on their faces. Other than that they look much like miniature versions of people. Now, the thing about brownies is they don't have proper surnames when they're born."

"Why not?" asked Alfred.

"It's just the way brownies are, they're proud folk and prefer to make it on their own. So, instead of each father passing his surname on to his children, the young brownies must find their own surname. And before you ask how, I'll tell you. Brownies have to earn their surnames by doing something for a human. I see you're still confused. Have you ever heard the story about the old cobbler who was working on a fancy pair of shoes and fell asleep with them unfinished?"

"Yes," replied Alfred.

"Well, as most people tell the story who is it that helps the old cobbler?"

"Elves, I always heard it was elves."

"And that is where everyone gets it wrong, it was not elves that helped the old cobbler, but brownies and that old cobbler was more then likely none other than Alfgar's father. You remember Alfgar, the lad in the story about the goblin attack on this very city. Very good. Anyway, on top of all this Father Christmas's helpers aren't elves, elves aren't even tiny, no, Father Christmas's helpers are brownies."

"Really?" said Alfred with excitement in his eyes.

"Yes, really. Now then, the brownies had been watching for some time to see if there wasn't a way they could earn their names, and this was it. "The old man has finished carving the sign, it simply needs to be painted we could become Painters and have our surnames, finally," said Alan, who was the leader of this small group of brownies. The brownies agreed that this was their best chance, so after Henry Bucklin fell asleep they sneaked into his room in the tavern and finished painting the sign for him. They toiled all through the night creating beautiful colors as only a brownie can. You see brownies, as soon as they set to a task, become extremely efficient at it. It's why a brownie must choose carefully what job they want to do, because once they choose they'll only be good at that job and it is very hard for them to change vocations, but that is a story for another time.

"The following morning, when Henry awoke, he looked down and saw the finished sign. 'I must have finished it during the night and have forgotten about it,' said Henry to himself. Now this greatly angered the brownies—"

"Why?" asked Alfred.

"Well, you see lad, there are actually two parts to a brownie's receiving his surname. The first is doing something helpful for a human. The second, however, is the human thanking the brownie or brownies involved by acknowledging their work as their own, or simple confusion over who has done all the work for him. When Henry did neither, but assumed he had finished the work, the brownies grew outraged because they had not-received their surnames. 'All right lads,' said Alan in a hushed voice. 'If this old codger isn't going to recognize us as the finishers of his work then we'll have to cause him some mischief.'

"I highly recommend, if you can ever help it, lad, never anger a brownie. He takes on many impish tendencies when you do and he will find a way to cause you harm or at least extreme annoyance.

"Well, for the first week or so after the brownies had finished Henry's sign, things went well for him, people were frequenting the Tarnished Bell, travellers liked the rooms enough to recommend them to others, every-thing was running smoothly. It was at the height of his success that the brownies struck.

"It started with a few horses getting knots in their tails, right outside the Tarnished Bell. Then horses' shoes would come loose while they were tied up outside of the Tarnished Bell. When this did not produce the desired effect, the brownies decided to make matters worse. 'Here's what we'll do,' said little Alan the brownie, 'we'll start breaking the wheels of both passing and standing carts in front of the tavern,' and break them they did. Men would come out of the tavern and find all of their spokes broken. Carts that were driven past the tavern would first have their horses spooked and then the cart would come crashing down as the wheels shattered under their own weight. Upon inspection, they would notice tiny little nicks in the spokes. The brownies used the little knives that all brownies keep to do the dirty work."

"Why do brownies keep little knives?" asked Alfred.

"They keep the knives much like we do pocketknives, you never know when one might come in handy. The only difference is that a brownie's knife is much stronger and sharper than our pocketknives and can cut through almost. anything. Now where was I?"

"The brownies were using their knives to cut the spokes of cartwheels."

"Ah yes, this caused Henry much trouble, as he was unsure as to the reason of these occurrences. On top of that, patrons of the tavern visited less often and most. spoke of the tavern as the home of the broken spokes.

"Henry was unsure of how to handle this problem and called upon Alfgar to help him. While these events took place before the great Goblin attack, Alfgar was still noted as an individual who understood these strange occurrences. 'Alfgar, my friend, I'm at a loss, I don't know what's going on.'

"'I've seen this before,' said Alfgar. 'So have you, Henry.'

"'I have?' questioned Henry.

"'Yes, Henry, remember a few years ago when my father, Hedley, had problems with the shoes he was making? The stitching would come undone as people walked away. Sometimes as they put on their new shoes, they would go to leave the store and find their shoes had been tied together by the lacing. It was awful.'

"'Yes, yes, I remember. What happened, had your father angered some spirits?'

"'Spirits? Not exactly. Brownies. Father went to sleep one night working on a particularly difficult pair of boots for the mayor and they were to be finished by morning. Well, a couple of brownies undertook it to help my father. In the morning, he assumed that he or I, without remembering, finished the boots and thought no more about it. This made the brownies angry, so they plagued the devil out of my father until he realized what happened.'

"'What did he do? How did he get them to stop?'

"'Simple, he walked up to the mayor and told him that brownies had finished the boots. The mayor was confused, but my father was adamant and that was enough for the brownies. In your case, however, more drastic measures may be needed.'

"'I'll do whatever it takes to make the little devils stop.'

"'I wouldn't recommend you start by calling them names, they're no more related to demons or angels than you or I. Anyway, here's what we must do. You say that they have been breaking the spokes of your customers' and passers' by carts and wagons?'

"'Aye, that they have. It's gotten so bad some people are beginning to call my tavern home of the broken spokes.'

"'That's it. That's perfect.'

"'What is? Tell me, please, Alfgar.'

"'We'll rename the tavern. Tonight, you and I shall make a new sign for the new name of your tavern.'

"The following day, when people heard the old tarnished bell being wrung to announce the opening of the tavern, they were astounded at what they saw. Below the sign of the Tarnished Bell hung a new sign, that of a cartwheel with a broken spoke. The people were confused and when they asked Henry he simply said, 'Credit where credit is due.'

"It's said that Henry later met with the Painter brownies and that they made him a new sign in place of both the one they made and the one Alfgar and Henry put together, and that that is the sign we see today protected by the brownies' magic from wear and tear.

"It's also said that Henry made a deal with the Brownies never to change the name of the tavern out of respect for them.

"And there you have it lad, the story of The Broken Spoke Brownies."

Alfred was delighted with the story and he clapped loudly. His parents smiled, loving that the inn they had purchased not long after arriving in Carlisle was so storied. Life went on in much this way for some time, Alfred telling stories of seeing all manner of fantastical creatures in the forest, and Mr. Cyning telling them fairy-stories about the village of Carlisle. It was not, however, to last.

Chapter 2

Alfred was often teased when he spent time with other boys and girls his own age, especially as he grew older. The age of twelve was particularly difficult for Alfred. Nearly a teenager and having some of his friends and schoolmates already in their teens, it was deemed inappropriate by them when Alfred continued to profess belief in Father Christmas. Already in secondary school things progressively got worse as the cruelty of some of his schoolfellows increased with age.

He often found himself with his things spilled all over the ground, having them knocked out of his hands when he mentioned elves or fairies. Alfred had one friend through all of this: a young girl in his year, Winifrid Wendelyn. She would listen with rapt attention to the stories of Mr. Cyning, whether told by the old man himself or by Alfred. But even one friend can sometimes not be enough to deal with bullying.

Alfred's parents were worried. They decided it was perhaps best if Alfred spent a little less time with his godfather. Mr. Cyning continued to tell stories in the pub, but they usually kept Alfred busy during those times.

The forest remained one of Alfred's only escapes, but even it had become less of the safe haven he once remembered. He often took Wini with him, but she did not like it much. Alfred couldn't blame her. The forest had changed. It began to feel colder to him: not colder in temperature, but less friendly. If Alfred continued to see things in the forest he kept it to himself now. Whether Wini ever saw anything during their trips, she did not say. There were times, however, when his parents were uncertain whether it was a fear of bullies or a fear of the forest that kept him quiet. Things came to a head one day when Alfred came home babbling like a madman.

As Alfred and Wini walked home from the forest one day in the Autumn, he looked around at his surroundings, taking in the beautiful outdoors. Carlisle is a wonderful town to see in the early stages of autumn. The leaves had already turned their different colors and were beginning to fall. The sidewalk upon which they were strolling was particularly leaf strewn. Had it not been, he might not have heard the sound of someone walking behind him. Alfred quickened his pace. Alfred had been told that certain creatures only come out at night, but the sun was slowly setting. "If we can only make it to the corner, we'll be home free," Alfred thought. He grabbed Wini's wrist and began to run. Just around the corner was his house where he could shout for his mother and father to come out and greet him as he came home. Then something quite unusual happened.

Just before they reached the corner, with the footsteps behind them quickening in the leaves, Alfred found a sudden boost of bravery. He let go of Wini's hand, ran, slid in the leaves as he stopped, about-faced and started to run in the other direction, toward whoever, or whatever, was following him. Alfred closed his eyes, involuntarily, as he made for the one following him. Thus, he did not see that nothing was behind him. As he continued to run, however, he opened his eyes just in time to trip ripping his pants and scraping his knee on the sidewalk. "Who tripped me?" Alfred exclaimed, as he sat on the concrete, nursing his wound. When no reply was returned, Alfred stood up and limped back home, not noticing a slight rustling in the bushes, nor the large ring of mushrooms next to him that bordered the side of the inn. Wini was crying, her wrist was hurt. They gave her some ice, and some ice cream, and called her parents. The Wendelyns collected their daughter and Alfred saw very little of her after this.

His parents did not know what to do with him once he got home. "I was chased by a something, I think it was a goblin," he shouted as his parents tried to calm him down. "How can I calm down? I'm telling you, something was after me. I need to see Mr. Cyning." His parents looked concerned.

"I'll go get him," his father said at last. It would not be quite right to say that in this moment George believed his son. Neither, however, would it be quite right to say that he did not. George was confused.

Jessica was no better off. Torn between her own early belief in Mr. Cyning's stories and the pragmatism that began to set in as she settled down into family life in a family run pub, she wanted to believe her son and also to believe that evil things such as goblins could not possibly exist. She was able to console Alfred eventually, when the adrenaline wore off. She cared for his cuts, fixed him some tea and sat quietly with him awaiting her husband's return.

Several hours went by and Jessica sat with her son in silence, holding him closely. Finally, she heard keys in the lock. The door opened and there stood Mr. Cyning and her husband. She noticed the look on her husband's face was one of confusion, or perhaps better, uncertainty. He took her aside, "I think we should leave those two alone. Come with me and I'll tell you what Mr. Cyning said." What it was Mr. Cyning told his father, Alfred could not hear. He had, instead to focus his attention on Mr. Cyning who had now sat himself opposite Alfred.

"Alfred, my dear child, your father told me about the fright you had today," he said slowly and sadly.

"It was a goblin, Mr. Cyning, I'm almost sure of it. It was chasing me down the lane. I thought they couldn't be out in sunlight. I thought it killed them or something. You always say that they hate sunlight, but this one didn't. Or maybe it was something else, are there other evil things in the forest?" Alfred's eyes were wide, his voice quick.

"Yes, there are other evil things in this world. Alfred," he said looking intensely at the boy, "we need to spend some time apart. It's too dangerous. Today you could have—" he stopped, tears seemed to be welling in his eyes. "You're getting too old to believe in my stories, Alfred. It's time for you to move on from them."

"But I don't want to. I believe, Mr. Cyning, I believe in your stories."

"Stay away, boy. For now you must stay away. But never stop believing." He added in a whisper. If Mr. Cyning realized he just contradicted himself, he did not let on. He simply walked out of the inn.

Alfred, near-teenager though he was, wept. His parents tried to console him as best they could, but for weeks Alfred did little but go to school and come home again. He began to play video games and watch television, reading only occasionally and mostly for school. It took months before he ventured back into the forest. His mother began sending him for mushrooms every now again, going with him the first few times and then sending him on his own. It was even months before Mr. Cyning started telling stories at the inn again. When he did, Alfred, if not already otherwise occupied, would go to his room. Wini he altogether neglected. It was not her fault they did not speak much after the incident, or at least not wholly. She tried to talk to him about fairies, but Alfred would put on a superior air and say something about kid's these days. She often went to the inn to see Alfred and listen to Mr. Cyning's stories. She saw little of Alfred, but she drank in the old man's stories. Life, for Alfred, continued this way for many years.

Chapter 3

Alfred had been home for several months and winter was fast approaching when one morning, well before sunrise, Alfred's mother knocked on his bedroom door, "Alfred, would you be a dear, and go into the wood to fetch me some of the mushrooms for my mushroom soup? It's rained overnight and there ought to be a fair few to be had." Jessica Perkins's mushroom soup was famous several miles around Carlisle, particularly for its rarity and freshness. Jessica only used a certain kind of mushroom, and then only fresh picked. Alfred stumbled out of bed, pulling on trousers and a jumper his mother knit for him last Christmas; it being a chilly morning. Alfred had a quick bite of toast and glug of coffee and went out into the mist.

It is about two miles from Alfred's home to the edge of Fey Forest, so Alfred had to walk by the old church St. Nicholas's, which had burn marks on the stones still from some attack back in the late middle ages or early renaissance. Alfred could never remember. Local history did not interest him too much, and no one could settle on the date anyway. Some said it happened during the reign of Queen Elizabeth when some of the old Catholic churches were being burnt down. Others said it was during the time of Oliver Cromwell. Still others said it was a much more ancient and diabolic attack from early in the church's history. Whatever the truth was, no renovation was allowed since it was deemed a historical landmark.

When Alfred reached the forest's edge the mist became even worse. "It's going to be damn near impossible to find mushrooms in this mist," he said to himself. "Oh well, in I go." With that he plunged into the wood. The trees were close together in this small wood and blocked out whatever sunlight might be burning the mist off outside of it. Alfred put his headphones in his ears and was listening to music as he searched, none too carefully.

He yawned, another thirty minutes and he would simply give up and tell his mother there were no mushrooms yet. Off in the distance Alfred saw a light. As he walked closer to it, he could tell it was several lights, as if from torches. Wondering what on earth could be going on he decided to walk towards them.

If Alfred had not had his headphones in he would have been surprised still to be hearing music. He would have heard music that could leave no listener unmoved. It was both morose and jovial. It sounded both as if it were the music of another world and yet as if it were the rocks, trees, streams, Nature herself singing this song. But all Alfred could hear was his own music pulsing through his ears as he walked ever closer to the torches, looking like phantoms of red and orange in the mist.

Although Alfred could not hear the merry voices and beautiful music, he could smell the food: roasted meat, delightfully prepared vegetables, and wine. The mist obscured his sight even more as he ventured closer. He was quite near the torches and could almost taste the food when suddenly all the torches vanished. The dark enclosed his senses and he fell.

"I must have fallen asleep," said Alfred out loud as he pulled his headphones out of his ears and stowed them in his pocket. He looked around confused. "Well," he thought, "I must have been more tired than I realized this morning. Imagine me thinking there was a party going on out here in this mist, this early in the morning." He looked around for any signs, but all he saw was a fairy ring, mushrooms in a perfect circle with one enormous mushroom directly in the middle.

"Well, today's my lucky day," Alfred said. "Just the mushrooms Mum needs for her soup. I think I'll grab this big one first." Alfred reached down, but as he did so he knocked the top off the mushroom before he even got his hands round its base.

"That's not a very kind way of introducing yourself, knocking off my hat, Alfred Perkins." Alfred looked around. "Down here, my son. My how you humans persist in not seeing what's right before you. I said down here." Alfred could not believe what his eyes beheld. Standing before him not more than two feet off the ground was a brown, dry looking figure with a sort of green tunic and shoes on. It had almost no nose and its eyes were a loam brown, and it appeared to have no teeth or discernible ears. All Alfred could see at the moment, however, was a talking mushroom without its cap.

"Well, it seems I will have to re-collect my own hat. Oh, and don't be worried, my son, you are not dreaming. I promise you I am quite real. My name is—" The creature bent over to pick up its cap and Alfred took his chance and ran.

Alfred ran past several other collections of mushrooms, shuddering as he did. "I was still half asleep," he told himself. "I couldn't find any mushrooms, laid down, and fell asleep dreaming of fires and talking mushrooms. Yes, that's it. There can't be such things as talking mushrooms. There just can't." Alfred stopped running when he reached the church. He needed to collect his thoughts before he got back home. He decided to tell his mother that it was too soon after the rain for there to be any mushrooms yet.

"Well, no mushroom soup today, then," his mother said when he arrived back at home. "You look a little put out, why don't you lay back down."

"That's alright, I'll go see if Dad needs me in the brewery."

Alfred went down into the brewery where he found his father next to a large wooden beer barrel. "Alfred!" He shouted. "Just in time, my boy. I was about to do a little taste test. I've got a new amber ale I want you to try." Alfred's father took great pride in his beer. It was part of what gave The Broken Spoke its charm, all house brewed cask ale. Alfred was lost in thought. He wandered out of the cellar, leaving his father to his brewing revelries and spent the rest of the day in a kind of a stupor. He helped his parents in the garden, milked the cows, fed the chickens and served in the inn at night.

Alfred was collecting mugs and pint glasses outside when he saw him. Old Mr. Cyning was sitting outside, as he had to nowadays, smoking his pipe. "How old is he now?" Alfred thought to himself. "He seemed ancient when I was a little kid." Old Mr. Cyning was old indeed, probably the oldest member of the village of Carlisle. If you wanted to know anything about the history of Carlisle or Britain in general he was the man to ask. He could tell you stories about Alfred, Merlin, and Gildas; or about Churchill and the War. He noticed Alfred staring at him, took a big puff on his pipe, blew out a glorious smoke ring, tamped his pipe, placed it back between his teeth and said, "Bee in your bonnet, Alfred?"

"Just a bit distracted today, Mr. Cyning."

"Yes, I heard you fell asleep out in the woods. Right next to fairy ring, if young Sammy's eyes didn't deceive her."

"Oh, um, would mind not mentioning that to my mum. I was supposed to be collecting mushrooms for her soup—"

"Your mother makes a damn fine mushroom soup."

"Yes, well I was supposed to be collecting mushrooms, but I must've fallen asleep and had a terrible dream. When I woke up I forgot all about the mushrooms and ran straight back home."

"Oh," said Mr. Cyning. Taking a long draw on his pipe, he closed his eyes. Alfred thought he had fallen asleep when suddenly he heard Mr. Cyning murmur, "And what was your dream about?"

"Um," said Alfred nervously. "I can't really remember, mushrooms I think. A-a talking mushroom." Alfred did not want to say too much. He was not sure which frightened him more, the idea that people might here him, or that Mr. Cyning would believe him. Oliver Cyning was well known for believing the unbelievable. He had a reputation that inspired both a kind of reverence at the breadth of his knowledge and an incredulity at the things he found credulous, as Alfred well knew.

"Damn," swore Mr. Cyning.

"Sorry?" Alfred replied.

"My pipe's gone out. Can you see if your mum or dad have any matches I can borrow?"

"Sure," said Alfred. Not at all unhappy to have the subject changed. Or so he thought at first. When Alfred returned with the matches Mr. Cyning was gone. Alfred could not help feeling a little let down. It would have been nice, as well as terrifying, to have Mr. Cyning believe he really saw a talking mushroom. Alfred thought back to those days as a child when he listened to and believed every word Mr. Cyning said. A small part of him missed those days.

That night, as Alfred drifted off to sleep he really did have a dream, but not about talking mushrooms. He was walking in Fey Forest when he saw the torches again. This time they were much clearer. He could hear the music as well. The music made him feel brave, but sad, as if he was meant to be the last defender of a dying cause. It gave him the kind of courage not to overcome insurmountable odds, but to be defeated with dignity and hope. The music was nothing, however, to the people he saw there. They were pure beauty: men and women, feasting, laughing, singing, drinking, looking as though the belonged to a medieval tapestry rather than the woods just outside a twenty-first century village. Their clothes were magnificent, bright blues and greens and golds, reds and yellows, no color seemed missing. Yet the clothes were not ostentatious, nor opulent. They were the colors of the woods themselves in early summer when everything was blossomed.

As Alfred drew nearer he found that he could not quite make out what they were saying. It seemed clear that they spoke English and yet the dream kept him from comprehension. Suddenly the scene changed. The lights of the beautiful people turned blue. Stern, determined looks washed over their merry faces. Weapons were drawn by men and women alike: bows and arrows, swords, clubs, knives, daggers, lances, axes. Horses appeared, as if commanded, but Alfred saw no one go for them or call for them. Some mounted, others remained standing and they went forward as if for battle. What happened next was a complete mystery for just as the enemy of the beautiful people was about to appear, Alfred awoke.

"Alfred, dear," he could just discern his mother calling, "you said you would look for mushrooms again today."

"Be right out, Mum," he mumbled in reply.

Alfred splashed cold water on his face, dressed and went out into another misty morning. He took his time walking to forest. Whether it was because of the dream or being woken up suddenly he could not decide, but he left his headphones behind. Alfred stopped to look at the church as the sun was just beginning to rise over its steeple.

"Have I ever told the story of how this church was nearly burnt down?" said a familiar voice behind him.

"Mr. Cyning," said Alfred both startled and relieved, "where did you go yesterday? When I came back to bring you your matches you had gone."

"Hmm? Oh, I found some in my pocket and had a sudden urge to take a walk in the forest."

"You did?"

"Yes, your story had me interested. I believe you told your mother there were no mushrooms, yes?"

"Yes," Alfred said a little dejectedly. "I didn't want her to think me mad for running scared out of the forest."

"Mmhmm. Is that where you're headed now?"

"It is. She really wants those mushrooms."

"Would you mind if I joined you? I do like a good walk in the morning."

"Sure," Alfred replied, hoping for an opportunity to discuss his latest dream.

"You know," Alfred said slowly, "I don't think you have ever told me your version of what happened to St. Nicholas's."

"Oh! Well then, you are in for a treat." Alfred only half-listened while he and Mr. Cyning walked closer to the woods. He thought he must be hearing him wrong, for when he would occasionally tune back in he heard words like goblins, trolls, feys. He thought Mr. Cyning must have started in on a fairy tale.

"No, Mr. Cyning," Alfred said exasperatedly. "I mean the real story of what happened to the church." However, as Alfred said this he turned and noticed that Mr. Cyning was no longer next to him. He found himself lost in a fog in the forest. "Now where did Mr. Cyning get to? Where did I get to, for that matter? It wasn't this foggy when I got up this morning." Alfred looked around but did not recognize where he was in the forest. He kept trudging forward, occasionally shouting "Mr. Cyning!" thinking the old man had gotten lost in the fog as well.

Alfred walked for what seemed hours, knowing that the right thing to do was to stay in one place and wait for the fog to clear but being unable to do so. It was as if something was drawing him further and further into the forest. Suddenly, as if a veil had been lifted, Alfred saw before him the torchlights, just as he had yesterday morning and in his dream. This time there was no music. He could make out the sounds of voices, but could neither see their owners nor understand them clearly. The tone, however, was clear: anger. It was a stern anger, even a proper anger, but it was anger nonetheless. The whole forest seemed full of it.

Alfred proceeded as quietly as he could, moving ever closer. He began to make out the forms of those speaking. They were the beautiful people from his dream. He was staring in disbelief as he continued to edge closer when suddenly SNAP. Alfred trod on a small twig. The torches disappeared in an instant and everything went dark.

Alfred awoke on the ground, once again next to a circle of mushrooms. He was feeling himself to make sure no permanent damage was done when he heard a voice nearby. At first he thought it was Mr. Cyning. "Thank goodness," he said aloud. "I thought I would never find you."

"I've been here the whole time."

"Well, at least we're together again. Maybe now we can find our way out of the blasted forest."

"Oh I don't know about that. Who would watch over my mushrooms?"

In horror did Alfred turn around to see the thing to which the voice belonged. It was the talking mushroom again. "B-but—" he stammered.

"You're not going to knock my hat off again, are you, my son?" asked the mushroom.

Alfred's head was swimming. A blackness descended on his eyes. He could just hear the voice saying, "Goodnight" as his head hit the ground and Alfred knew no more.

Chapter 4

Alfred woke slowly, barely opening his eyes, too afraid of what he might see. Once they were opened, he was relieved. He was no longer in the forest. He was in what looked like an old cottage. "Good, you're awake. You gave me a right turn, boy," said a voice in the distance. This time Alfred was quite sure it was Mr. Cyning's voice. This, however, gave no immediate reassurance. Alfred's mind was suddenly flooded with questions: Where was he? How did he get there? How long had he been unconscious? All of these questions he put to Mr. Cyning.

"One thing at a time, boy. Here, drink some of this." He handed Alfred a glass. It tasted like wine but was earthier and drier than any wine he had ever had before. Alfred drank quietly, hoping Mr. Cyning would answer all or any of his questions. Mr. Cyning went out back, into what Alfred could only assume was his garden. Alfred sat looking around, trying to take in his surroundings. He was on a couch in what looked like the sitting room of an old stone cottage. The walls were lined with bookshelves, there were even books on the mantlepiece over the fireplace. Books of history, philosophy, mythology, fairy tales, medieval manuscripts, old books of theology, even some fiction and children's stories seemed to be included in this antiquated library.

Whatever it was Mr. Cyning was doing in his garden, he came back in smiling, but there was a concerned look in his eyes. "Well, boy, how are you doing?" was all he said. Alfred's head began screaming with questions. Again he tried to get Mr. Cyning to answer them. The old man seemed reluctant, as if he wished not to say too much or too little. Alfred looked at the old man, pleading for answers with his eyes. "It's time you know," Mr. Cyning said slowly. At last, Alfred was going to get some answers.

"Come with me out into the garden, bring your wine," he told Alfred. They walked outside, the sun assaulted Alfred's eyes. "Passing out two days in a row isn't helping you keep your feet, is it?" said Mr. Cyning as Alfred stumbled.

"I'm fine, just a little weak still."

"Well, keep drinking that wine." Mr. Cyning produced a loaf of bread and the two of them sat out in his garden under the shade of a large weeping willow facing Fey Forest. In the distance Alfred could just make out the mountain rising high above the forest. Mr. Cyning produced a pipe, tobacco, and some matches from his various pockets. Puffing slowly he turned to Alfred, "It's all true, boy."

"W-what do you mean?" asked Alfred terrified of the answer.

"The dreams, the ancient one you've met in the forest, the torches, all of it is true. I know, it sounds ridiculous, but it's true all the same. Faërie is all around us. The world is so much bigger than you've dreamt of. It's like what Hamlet told Horatio, there's more in heaven and earth than are dreamt of in your philosophies.

"Look, Alfred, I'll be honest with you, elves, gnomes, dwarves, goblins, giants, dragons they're all real. The ones who are good are better than you could ever imagine, but the wicked are darker than anything. Most people live their whole lives thinking Faërie is just another word for imagination or the supernatural. They never get the chance to see. Ah, we've been cursed with blindness for so long now. Not that Faërie has ever been easy to see, far from it, but we weren't meant to be completely ignorant of it. Arthur knew Faërie, this wood was named after his half-sister, you know. Morgana was, well, she was confused she was. Robertus Kirk, MacDonald, Chesterton, Lewis, Tolkien, they all understood, they believed in Faërie, even if they infrequently got into it, they knew it was there. You're lucky, well, maybe that's the wrong word. You've been given a gift, you've spent your whole life on the edge of Elfland, as it were, and now you've stumbled in."

Alfred did not believe what he was hearing. Faërie? Elfland? Goblins, dragons, gnomes? No. He lived in a world where science had dispelled all those old beliefs. There was no way this could be true. Alfred was just about to say so when he noticed a ring of mushrooms right next to weeping willow. He let out a shriek he would have normally been ashamed of as suddenly an enormous mushroom from the centre of the circle began walking towards them. It removed its cap and wiped its brow, "Told him the truth at last, eh, Oliver? I told you you should have done it years ago. He would have believed you and I could have been left out of it."

"I know what I'm doing. I've been at this a long time, Balthazar."

"Of course, sir."

Alfred was still staring, though the horror he felt at first was beginning to transition to curiosity. Hadn't he always loved fairy tales and legends when he was a boy? It was at university he began to despise them in a fashionable exercise toward popularity. "What's going on? What, or I suppose I should say who, are you?"

"Balthazar Toadstool, historian and mushroom shepherd, which is to say a gnome, at your service." The gnome gave a bow.

"Alfred Perkins," Alfred mumbled out, still somewhat in shock.

"Gnomes are among the wisest creatures in Faërie, Alfred" said Mr. Cyning. "And old Balthazar here is accounted wise even by his own kind."

"You do me honour, sir," was the gnome's reply.

"What I really want to know," said Alfred, "is what the devil is going on?"

"You've been having dreams, haven't you, my son," said Balthazar. "Dreams about a wondrous folk in the forest. But your dreams have turned darker, haven't they? It's no surprise. Evil never really goes away, we'll never truly see the end of it in this life. You have been given a gift, my son, the gift of the second sight. All humans can see Faërie, or Elfland as many of us call it. They work at not seeing it. Even you tried not to see it, explaining away your dreams and the two times we have met, but unlike most humans you cannot not see Elfland. More than that, you have dreams of the goings on of Elfland. There's a darkness brewing, such as we have not known for a long age. It's been plaguing your world more than our own. All these wars you have been having, the hatred of humans for their brothers and sisters, but Elfland has been left relatively alone. We are the poorer for not having your world interact with ours, we grew static, but we endured in peace. Now, however, the evil plaguing your own world is making its way into ours.

"The dwarves first alerted us to it. They heard them in the deep recesses of the mountain, digging, coming in from goodness knows where. The dwarves, crafty as they are and even knowing the mountain as well as they do, cannot tell where they are or if they have come out. Your dreams tell us one thing, however, they are coming and they will bring destruction with them when they do."

Alfred sat in rapt attention. "Who is coming?" he asked, breaking the ominous silence.

"Goblins."

"I'm sorry. Did you just say goblins?"

"Yes, my son, goblins. Some of the fierce stand most wicked creatures ever to cross the face of the earth."

"What are they? I mean, I remember reading about them in books, but they're usually small mischievous little creatures, lesser demons or imps, awful for sure, but not this menacing."

"Yes, well did your books tell you that mushrooms were cared for by gnomes?"

"No."

"Then I would not use them as your guide through Elfland. That's what I'm for."

"Wait, what do you mean? Mr. Cyning, what does he mean, he's my guide through Elfland? If there are goblins in there and they're as bad as you say, shouldn't I stay out of it altogether?"

Mr. Cyning sighed heavily. Alfred in looking at him began to realize how very old, even careworn, the eccentric old man of Carlisle was. It was as if he was looking at him for the first time and rather than an old man, it was a wizard, a sage, druid bard sitting next to him. "Alfred," he began slowly, "Carlisle sits in a perilous place. While Faërie may be all around us and everywhere, there are some places closer to it than others. As I told you, you are quite lucky, having grown up on the edge of Elfland and being given a glimpse. A glimpse, however, is not all you've been destined for.

"Carlisle, because of its proximity to the major home for elves and dwarves, the elf kingdom and the lesser dwarf kingdom have their thrones in Fey Forest, has often known great beauty and wonder. Alas, it is also known more grief and woe."

"And caused more as well," said Balthazar quietly.

"Too true," replied Mr. Cyning. "Alfred, trouble has often come from Elfland and attacked Carlisle, trying to find entrance into the world of men and overthrow it. The goblins especially hate humanity. Do you remember the story I told you about St. Nicholas's?"

"Only a little. Didn't you say something about goblins then?"

"Indeed I did. They tried to burn down the church on Christmas Eve over a thousand years ago. They were beaten back by the villagers, with the help of the faeries, and the flames around the church were extinguished."

"Why did they want to burn down the church?"

"Suffice it to say that they hate humanity and wanted to do them harm. The whole village was inside at the time, as was the custom, and they thought to bring the whole town to ruin. From there they could have spread into the rest of the human world."

"Why do they hate us so much? And why do they have enter our world through Carlisle?"

"Those are complicated questions. Balthazar, would you mind answering the boy?"

"My pleasure. You see Alfred, goblins were not always goblins. Some say they are men mixed with elves who have gone bad. Others that they were elves once, but they turned their backs on their own. Still others say they were dwarves who lost themselves in the mines they worked for the elves and when they finally emerged it was with a burning hatred of the elves. Whatever the truth is, they were not always evil and they did not always look as they do now. The reason they hate humanity is because the Elfin King and Queen protect you. It is because of them that goblins and other wicked creatures cannot come into your world unless your civilisation is physically close to our own. Because humans have moved away from the forests and the wilds of the world, even from the beginning, this happens rarely, but there are still pockets. In most places there is still silence, in some evil has won out, but here in Carlisle there is ever a tension. The greater and lesser kingdoms being here means both a greater chance of mutual benefit and a greater chance of mutual harm."

"So where do I fit in to all of this?"

Balthazar and Mr. Cyning looked to each other and then both turned to look at Alfred. Mr. Cyning spoke first, "Faërie is always better when connected to humanity. The separation between the two is unnatural. When evil like this comes forward is important for Faërie to find a human with the second sight to help. What your proper role will be, cannot yet be told. This is why Balthazar is to be your guide. Whatever part you are called to play, it will be a great one, lad, I can promise you that."

"Come along, my son," Balthazar said to Alfred.

"Wait, I'm leaving now? What about my family?" Alfred exclaimed.

"There's no time, boy. The goblins will come and attack the village. If you don't go into Faërie now, there may be no Carlisle to return to. I know its hard. I had hoped to better prepare you myself, but there we are. Alfred, the goblins are ruthless, their king hates humanity more than most. He comes from a long-lived goblin line and was part of the attack against the village when they tried to burn St. Nicholas's. He will stop at nothing. He's been biding his time far in the North, for they were banished from England for a thousand years, all that time to foment and plan for his revenge. A young villager caved in part of his face with a mattock, and since then he has vowed revenge against humanity for the loss of his eye, not to mention a fair few of his teeth. He will have trained his goblins to be ferocious, cruel, loving to give pain. You must go, and now."

Alfred remembered the music from his dream, he thought of how much he loved his parents, his village. He was confused, about so many things, but one thing was certain, he trusted Mr. Cyning, everything he read about Faërie, all of it incidental, taught him to discern good from evil. He knew evil must be fought, even in the face of defeat, which he hoped it would not come to. Without realising it, he found himself resolved to do whatever he could. He could think of nothing that made him special, that made him worthy, but this too he knew so often essential in fairy tales. It was not about him, but what needed to be done.

"Alright," he said at last, "I'll do it. Lead me where you will Balthazar."

"Into the forest then, my son."

"Good luck, Alfred," called Mr. Cyning. "The hopes of Faërie and England rest with you."

Alfred looked changed, as if the air of Elfland had already begun to flow in him. His walk became more determined, less that of a listless twenty-something, as he entered the forest, being guided by the small gnome, not knowing what his fate would bring him.

Chapter 5

As Alfred and Balthazar ventured deeper into the wood, Alfred noticed a change. The air seemed richer, more fulfilling, the colors seemed more vibrant. "That's the air of Elfland you're breathing in, my son," Balthazar said without turning around, as if he knew what kinds of affects it was having on Alfred. "For most humans it makes them confused, it's why they get lost. For seers, however, it has the opposite effect. You will feel your senses getting clearer, sharper. Goodness becomes amplified in the good, badness in the bad." This made Alfred afraid and so he checked the pride beginning to swell in his heart.

"Can non-seers ever be taught to see?" he asked the gnome.

"Not in the way you do. They can never see dreams of Elfland, or anywhere else for that matter. They can, however, be taught to see Elfland with their waking eyes. The air here can have the same effect on them. Even when it does confuse it almost always has a positive effect on those who breathe it. But while true seers are born, great seers are first born and then made."

Alfred pondered this. "You mean the ability is innate, but its application must be practiced."

"Tried would be truer, but yes, that is the general idea. You must learn how to see with the sight you have been given."

"How will I learn?"

"By patience, by exposure to Elfland, and by telling me all you see in dreams."

They marched on for several more hours, with no sign of relenting. It was now that Alfred realized Balthazar was not walking on top of the ground, but wading through the forest floor as if it were water. "Is that how you always walk?" he asked, hoping he was not being impolite.

"Gnomes are at home in the dirt in nearly the same way fish are in water. Or perhaps more like whales, we do not draw our breath from the earth, but we swim and glide through it. It is our home."

They continued on in silence. Balthazar stopped. At first, Alfred thought he had offended the gnome with an impertinent question. Balthazar, however, turned to Alfred and whispered, "Go stand behind one of these trees, and be quiet. I'll be back shortly." With that, Balthazar burrowed into the dirt, or perhaps dove better describes his entrance into the earth so that he vanished from Alfred's sight.

Alfred did his best to remain quiet as he moved behind one of the trees. He heard voices in the distance and a loud plodding as if feet which were marching to different beats were trying to keep pace with one another. He crouched down behind a tree and held his breath. What he saw frightened him, and had he not been in Elfland for many hours now, he might have fainted from fear. As it was, it took all of his courage not to scream and run away.

Lumbering before him—standing perhaps four and half feet high and three feet broad, with arms that would drag on the ground if not folded, skin a muddy mixture of black, brown, and green, eyes fierce and large, and teeth razor sharp—were two goblins. From how very wicked they looked did Alfred guess rightly that they were goblins.

"Ar, I hate walking in the sun, even if the trees are dense. It hurts my eyes and makes me feel too warm," said one goblin to the other.

"You'd hate the punishment you'd get if refused to do your duty," replied the other.

"That's the truth of it. Oh, I can't wait to be done. We'll take over that mountain and never have to venture into the sun again, except when we want to torture someone. Oh it will be nice."

"Keep your voice down, you idiot. We're in enough danger as it is."

"I still say you were smelling things as weren't there, Hogsnout."

"And I'm telling you, I smelt human, and a human this close to those accursed elves and dwarves will do us no good. I promise you that. My nose has never failed and I tell you there was human nearby. If the smell's getting dimmer it either means he's spent too much time in this accursed place and is beginning to smell like it or he's gone. Neither option is good for us, nor our mission."

"Well then let's get on with what we've come to do. Do you think they'll join us?"

"Oh I'm sure of it. Our king will offer them land, and plenty of human and elfin flesh to eat. The trolls and giants will be on our side, no worries there. The hobgoblins may be harder to convince. Anyway, let's move on. You're right about one thing, whatever's happened with that human, our best bet is to finish with our mission and get back."

The two goblins hurried off, making more racket than was probably good for them. Alfred breathed a sigh of relief and then jumped with a start when he felt something tapping him on the shoulder. He grabbed stick nearby him and swung as he jumped away from whatever it was that accosted him.

"There you go, knocking my hat off again. I shall have to make a new one, or have the brownies do it for me, before my time with you is done," said Balthazar as he picked up his crumpled hat and dusted it off.

"So the goblins have found their way out of the mountain. Things are far worse than I feared." Balthazar soon began mumbling to himself, "Going to get trolls and giants? Things are worse, far, far worse than any of us have imagined. What are we going to do? What am I going to do with the boy? So much for the wisdom of the gnomes." He said finally as he sat down next to Alfred.

"Is it really so bad?" Alfred asked, breaking the silence.

"My son, Elfland has been at a relative peace for the past 300 years. Now war is upon us and we are so near to being caught unawares that anything we can do or have planned up to now is just as likely to fail as to succeed."

What can I do? thought Alfred to himself. After all, he was just one man, and a young one at that. He had never been trained to fight and only found out all of this was real this morning. Still, it could be exciting, fighting against the forces of evil, protecting his village, really his whole world from the evils of Elfland. He would be remembered as mythic hero, dying fighting back the advances of darkness like the last of the three-hundred Spartans at the battle of Thermopylae. Yes, to die in battle, a sword in one hand, a shield in another, a true warrior, one who had to look his enemy in the eye, to recognize goodness alongside evil and to fight on and to die fighting for what is right.

It was when he started to think of death that he noticed the forest had suddenly gotten very dark and that coming toward him was a small cavalcade. The music he had heard in his dream or a music very like it was playing.

"Hello, my brothers," called Balthazar to them.

"Hail, Balthazar!" said an elf who alighted from his horse and walked towards them while the others began to make camp. "Well met, faithful gnome. I see you have the young Seer with you. Word has traveled to us through the forest, that you were bringing him. We have also felt a darkness being awoken. Come, we shall eat and drink. Tonight we feast ere the morrow brings us joys or woe." Alfred noticed many things about this elf. He was tall, his dark hair was worn long, as was his beard. His clothes were a beautiful mixture of greens, reds, and browns. On his chest there were four beasts: a bear, a bull, a boar, and a lion, all rampant.

The elves prepared a feast, they had clearly been hunting and a large white deer was roasting over an open fire they had prepared. "Tell me, Carlyle," Balthazar said to the elf who had first approached them, "what are your plans? You have heard our news about the goblins. What are the Queen's orders?"

Carlyle drained his cup, "The Queen has given but two orders: help the dwarves and trust the Seer."

Me? thought Alfred to himself. Alfred could not help feeling small, even insignificant amongst all these faerie-folk. To ask questions and observe seemed to be the only things for which he was needed, and those qualities did not seem to be desired. The music still lived on in his chest, making him feel brave, but his bravery seemed completely unnecessary. As he turned over in his mind what had happened to him since yesterday morning, he began to wonder about the two times previous he had come upon, if not this very camp, then one exceedingly like it. "Please," he asked Carlyle, "could you tell me why the first two times I approached your camp, you vanished and I was left sleeping on the ground?"

"Well, lad," Carlyle responded, "the reasons are three. First, even in peace we rarely allow ourselves to be seen by mortals, let alone when danger is upon our very hearth. Second, we believed it too much for your introduction to our fine country to begin with a host of evils. Third, even if we had not, it was Balthazar's duty to meet you first. Come, we have feasted, we will sing and then rest, for tomorrow may bring yet more woe if it is true we now have trolls and giants with which to contend." Somehow, Alfred thought the idea of woe and battle was both pleasing and saddening to Carlyle. It was as if his hands longed to feel his sword and to fight for goodness, but that such measures were necessary grieved him beyond anything. So much Alfred could read in his face, it was as if that face could not conceal truth or emotion, but must always wear whatever it felt. Alfred wondered if this was simply true of elves or if his eyes simply saw more now that he was under the influence of the air of Elfland.

Whatever singing there was, Alfred remembered very little of it. As soon as the music began he felt himself getting dreary. A she-elf, also dressed in a warrior's garb, led him to a tent prepared for him. Alfred laid down without undressing and was instantly asleep. It was not, however, a restful or dreamless sleep.

As Alfred slept, he found himself awake, conscious, but unable to see. At first he thought he was blind, or that he was still in his tent with his eyes closed, so he pulled them open but still saw noting. He continued to worry that he was blind until in the distance he saw a fire. He felt relieved, he was not blind, he was dreaming, and it was the same as the old dreams of the elves. Something, however, was different this time. The ground beneath his feet felt more solid. He reached out his hands to feel for trees, but instead felt rock and stone. He stumbled as he walked, but made his way towards the fire.

Like in his previous dream, the world around Alfred, as it became brighter, remained fuzzy, indeterminate. Again he heard voices, but could not understand what they were saying. He stumbled closer to the fire, trying to make as little noise as possible. Still he almost shouted when he began to understand what was going on. The smell of burnt hair was in the air, and dark figures danced about the fire, while another figure, much smaller, was being turned over and over, as if on a roasting spit. The roasting figure shouted, not from pain it seemed, but anger. Alfred cursed his inability to see or hear clearly. One thing, however, was evident, the goblins were amassing in the mountain, and they had caught at least one dwarf and were torturing him.

Alfred woke with a start. He knew he needed to tell someone what he saw. However, as he stepped outside of his tent all he could hear were shouts and a thunder of feet and hooves. The first thing Alfred saw outside of his tent was Carlyle throwing a sword at his feet while using his own to battle a goblin. The joy left his eyes. Alfred saw a steeled demeanour. However much Carlyle might normally joy in arms, he had no joy in this fray. This was as far as Alfred was able to think, however, for soon enough the goblins started making their way to him. He unsheathed his sword and prayed he could find that bravery the song of the elves usually stirred in him.

Goblins were now completely overrunning the camp when Alfred felt the earth shake. Several goblins lay dead at his feet, though his mind could little remember how they had died. His sword was smeared with blood and he himself was covered in cuts and bruises. The shaking grew worse. One of the elves standing near Alfred cried "Ettin! Ettin!" It did not take Alfred long to understand this word. Wading and crashing through the trees came an ugly, fearsome, albeit stupidly so, looking creature. It stood nigh 19 feet high. "Giant," Alfred whispered to himself.

Swinging its mighty club, the giant began clearing a path in front of it. Indiscriminately it struck down both goblin and elf. Whether this was due to the malice that burned its heart or sheer stupidity is uncertain, but whenever anything got in its way the giant swiped it away into the distance with its club. Alfred could hear the goblins shouting to it, trying to control it. Heedless to their cries the giant kept moving forward, straight for Alfred.

"Run!" shouted the elf standing next to Alfred. "We are no match for this brute, you and I." Alfred, however, stood firm and so the elf stayed with him. Both of them, swords drawn charged at the giant. Alfred swung his sword at the giant's tree-trunk of a leg, but it glanced off. He had only one idea. Alfred turned the sword around so it pointed down and raised it high above his head and brought it down on the giant's foot. The giant howled with anger. "Puny creatures," it shouted and swiped its club directly into Alfred. The force with which Alfred was hit took the breath out of him and sent him flying high up into the air and far away from the battle.

When Alfred awoke the sun was shining. "That giant must have sent me a good ways from the battle," he said to himself. He felt his arms, legs, and chest to check for any broken bones. His arms and legs felt stiff but fine, his chest, however, was incredibly sore and it hurt when breathed. Probably broke a few ribs, he thought. But what was he to do now? Was it safe to call for the others? "Carlyle!" he shouted, "Balthazar! Carlyle! Mr. Cyning!" No one answered. He looked around, but could not recognize what part of the forest he was in. He walked, hoping to find someone or somewhere familiar. Eventually he found his way to a lake. He could not remember there being a lake in Fey Forest, but nothing surprised him now. He knelt at the lake with some difficulty, cupped his hand, filled them, and drank. The water was cool and refreshing. He immediately began to feel better.

The water felt so good on his hands and head that he decided a swim would do him nicely. How different Alfred was, if he could have stopped to think. Not even two days ago he would never have thought of stripping down to go for a swim in a lake, let alone do so after having battled goblins and a giant. He pulled off his clothes and found most of his cuts already beginning healing, but he was still covered in bruises and his chest still smarted something awful. He waded into the water and his body immediately began to relax. He could feel strength returning to his limbs. He felt well enough to try a proper swim. It stung his chest at first, but the more he swam the better he felt.

After about an hour of swimming all of Alfred's cuts and bruises seemed to be healed. Even his ribs, which he thought broken, only caused him a small amount of pain. Alfred got out of the water and dried himself by simply lying on the soft down of the grass. After a short rest, he got dressed, and suddenly all that had taken place before he landed near this lake returned to his memory. He girded his sword and was about to set out in search of the elves and Balthazar when he noticed a cottage nearby. He walked toward uncertain of what he would find inside. Stories from his childhood told him it could be a witch, an elf, a beautiful princess, or an ogress. He felt, however, braver than before. Perhaps it was the encounter with the giant or lasting effects from the lake, but he was ready to meet any challenge. He knocked at the door. "Hello!" he shouted. "Is anyone home?" An elderly woman answered the door.

Chapter 6

"Come in, young man. I can see by the sheen of your hair and your countenance that you have been swimming in my lake."

"Yes, it has had a wonderful effect on me. I feel almost fully well, though my chest seems to pain me still." He looked around the inside of the woman's cottage. It was homely, but goodly so. It brought to mind home and hearth, the kind of things one wants to return to after a long journey. The old woman was meanwhile busy in her kitchen.

"Here," she said, returning with a damp cloth. "This has been soaked in my lake and over it I have said a few good words. Wrap it about your chest under your clothes and leave it for the rest of the day. Then you shall be completely healed, albeit changed."

Changed? thought Alfred to himself. Whatever doubts he had were dispelled, however, when the woman continued, "Something must be done about those goblins young man, and as you are the Seer it seems only right that you ought to be the one to do something about them."

"I feel ready to do almost anything, so long as it is good, honest, and worthy of poetry," as the words left his mouth, Alfred marvelled at himself. Did he really just said that? Was he desirous of being turned into a poem? He had always felt listless, little likely to do much of anything except in the service of his parents, and then usually with a fair bit of grumbling.

"You are surprised at yourself, I can tell. I may be old, but I can still see quite well."

"To tell you the truth, I am surprised. I have never sought adventure, never wanted to do anything brave. I just wanted to do something, something I loved, something that suited me."

"Did it never occur to you that what you wanted was to be good, honest, and poetical? Hmm? Did it never occur to you that this is what you wanted?"

Alfred thought back to all of old Mr. Cyning's stories. He had always felt invigorated after listening to Mr. Cyning. Knights saving princesses, slaying giants and dragons, paupers becoming princes because of their virtue. It was Mr. Cyning's stories that caused him to study literature at university. It was this study, however, that caused him to stop loving the stories, or so it seemed to him now. "Tell me, Lady," he said after reflecting, "is it the water of your Lake that has awakened this in me or the air of Elfland or the music of the Elves?"

"It is all three. No mortal can enter Elfland without becoming poetical unless they be too full of cynicism, none can hear the elfin songs without having even the smallest amount of bravery fanned into flame unless cowardice has too much hold on their heart. And none can swim in the waters of my Lake without having either their goodness or badness brought to the fore. Faërie makes the good things better, but exposes the bad for what it truly is."

Alfred briefly felt rather proud, but as the pride in him began to rise, the old woman stared hard at him and he heard in his mind, "but exposes the bad for what it truly is." He squelched that rising pride and turned his thoughts to finding the elves and stopping the goblins. "You will need to leave soon," said the old woman, "in order to stop the goblins."

"Indeed, I believe you're right, Mother," Alfred said turning to her. "Only I do not know which way to go. I have lost the elves and Balthazar Toadstool. Can you tell me, Mother, which is the best way for me?"

"The only way, Seer, to save Carlisle, the dwarves, and all of Elfland is to return from whence you came. Go back to the beginning and there you will find your answers."

Alfred was dejected. He did not wish to leave Elfland. He finally felt at home, finally felt as though he belonged in the world for the first time in his life. To return now, he feared, would cause him to disbelieve everything he had seen and experienced until now.

"My dear boy," said the old woman, "you do not belong forever in Elfland. Mortals are meant to live on the edges, living on the borders and entering in occasionally. When you started this journey, you simply wanted to save Carlisle, do not forget that."

Alfred knew that the old woman was right. He prepared to go immediately. "Hold on there, young man," she said suddenly. Alfred stopped as he was reaching for the door. "You will surprise people enough when you return without being dressed like the elves, openly carrying a sword." Alfred looked down and realized she was right. He could barely remember how he used to dress, though it had been only a few days, but despite the feelings he had always dressed this way, he knew this was not so. The woman pulled out of a closet somewhere the clothes he had worn when he entered the forest "Balthazar brought them to me," she said.

Alfred went into another room in the cottage. This room contained a small bed and a small mirror. He was surprised when he saw himself. The old woman's words caused him to expect to see big changes in himself. Instead he saw his beard starting to come in and his hair a bit matted. He found under the mirror a bowl of warm water, some soap, and a razor. He washed his hair and face, but decided to leave the beard, "It's the only reminder I'm going to have of my exploits here," Alfred said to himself. He changed his clothes, folded his elfin garments, and laid his sword on top, bringing them out to the old woman.

"You keep those," she said to him. "You never know when they might come in handy."

"Thank you," said Alfred with a little less rejection in his voice. With his things all packed in his rucksack, Alfred shouldered the bag and headed towards the door.

"Remember what I told you," the old woman called out behind him. "Go back to the beginning, only then can you save Elfland and Carlisle."

"I won't forget, Mother," he said turning around as he exited the door. The cottage, the old woman, even the lake was gone. Alfred was not surprised. He had faced giants and goblins, a fairy godmother was the last thing to surprise him now. And so Alfred sauntered on. Resolve and doubt mixed in him. In the end, what could he really do to stop an incursion of goblins. Surely the elves could take care of it without him. He would talk to Mr. Cyning when he got home, he would tell Alfred that it was his job to watch and not fight.

Hours went by and the forest began to grow more familiar. There was the tree he hid behind when he thought something was chasing him as a child. "I wonder if something was chasing me then?" He asked no one, who promptly answered in silence. As he walked on he noticed the ground began to be damp. Apparently it had rained in this part of the forest recently.

He kept a close eye out for mushrooms, hoping to find Balthazar. Instead he came upon a fairy ring of just the mushrooms his mother would want, but no shepherd guarding them. He picked them all, stowing them in his rucksack for his mother.

With no incident greater than finding the mushrooms, Alfred arrived at the edge of Fey Forest. He was disappointed. He had expected an attack, he had expected the elves or Balthazar or someone to arrive to divert his journey home a little while longer, but with no such luck. Perhaps the goblins were as yet unaware of him, or, as Alfred was beginning to believe, perhaps they simply felt him unimportant. With a sigh, Alfred stepped across the border separating the forest from the village and began to the two miles walk back home.

Chapter 7

Had Alfred not been deep in thought, and therefore completely oblivious to what was going on around him, he might have noticed that his walking through town was causing quite a stir. Old Mrs. Weatherby was leaning over whispering to her daughter, who then in turn ran across the street to the market to whisper to her best friend, a cashier called Evangeline, who told her manager, and so on. By the time Alfred reached The Broken Spoke, a crowd had gathered.

Alfred was pulled out of his contemplations by loud shouts. He was on the point of reaching into his rucksack for his elfin blade, thinking himself beset by goblins, when he realized it was simply the villagers of Carlisle. Some asked if he was OK, others sighed with relief. Alfred simply mumbled something about getting lost and needing sleep. His mother was soon in the midst of the crowd telling people either to come in and order something or to clear off. Alfred clearly needed his rest either way.

Once inside, however, his mother began to question him. "Where have you been? I could have died of fright when you didn't come home, especially after we heard you fainted out the woods a week ago."

"A week?" replied Alfred. "But I've only been gone for one night, two at most"

"Alfred, you've been gone for over a week. We were all so worried. Your father has put together a group to go searching for you in the woods."

"In Fey Forest!" Alfred exclaimed. "They can't. It's not safe in there right now. I have to go find Dad." Alfred grabbed his rucksack and began heading to the door when it opened and in stepped his father.

"I'm so glad your home," effused George. "Is it true, Jess, did he just come walking out of the woods this morning? Did you really, Son? Where have you been, what's happened? You look different, you need a shave for sure, but there's something else. Is everything alright, Son? What happened to you?"

Alfred's father released his embrace. Alfred looked at his parents. How could he tell them? How could he make them understand? "Nothing happened," he began. "I just got lost, is all. Has it really been a week?" He still could not believe it. Whether he had been passed out longer than he realized from his encounter with the giant, or time simply moved differently in Elfland, he could not be sure, but apparently he had been gone longer than he realized.

"Alfred," his mother said, "you know that forest like the back of your hand. Why you spent nearly every day in there when you were just a child."

"She's right, Son," said his father. "And there's something more, something I just can't quite put my finger on, something that's different about you. Tell us, Alfred, tell us what really happened. You can trust us."

Alfred was already feeling rotten about the deceit he was trying to employ. How could he lie to his parents who brought him up to be honest? Even if they would not, could not believe him. Even if they called him a liar or a lunatic he would have to tell them truth.

"Mum, Dad," he began, "you had better sit down. It all started, well what you tell me is a week ago, when you first sent me out to collect mushrooms. I didn't faint, and I wasn't so tired that I decided to take a nap. Something far stranger happened to me." And so Alfred proceeded to tell his parents what had happened to him. Everything from his first meeting with Balthazar, to Mr. Cyning's involvement, to battling the giant and the goblins with the elves and the old woman who cared for him. His parents were silent, and his father only got up to close the door before he returned to his seat and fixed his eyes on Alfred.

"Well, Jessica, it's finally happened. Just like he said it would," said Alfred's father to his mother. There was no pain in his voice, if anything it sounded like a mixture of resolution and joy.

"Yes, I'll fetch Mr. Cyning directly," replied his mother.

"So you mean, you believe me? You don't think I'm mad?"

"Son, have I ever told you how your mother and I met?"

"No," said Alfred. He wanted to say, "But I don't see what it has to do with anything," but his time in Elfland taught him to take nothing for granted.

"Your mother and I grew up in different towns, went to different universities, studied different things and were in no way likely to meet one another. Nevertheless, not long after we had each finished at university we both felt the need to travel. As you know, I'm from the South and your mother is from Scotland. When I decided I wanted to travel I headed north, she headed south. Both of us heard stories about an older man who lived in a little village called Carlisle. We neither of us thought much of it, but somehow both ended up in the same pub in Carlisle listening to the man tell a story.

"He said the story was called Alfred and the dragon, and all I can really remember about it now was that some Alfred who predated King Alfred had supposedly battled a dragon called Isengrim in Fey's forest. This Alfred was a member of Arthur's court and he, along with another knight called Carlyle defeated the dragon. I can't remember much else, right now, and perhaps Mr. Cyning can tell you himself, but that night I met your mother and fell in love. We both decided to stay in Carlisle. I took a job with the landlord of the pub we met in and she with the landlady. Before they died we got married and took over the pub from them when they retired. The Brandys were quite generous with us, having had no children of their own and left us everything in their will. The only proviso was to allow Mr. Cyning to come in and tell stories whenever he liked.

"Well, as I'm sure you'll believe, this was no problem for us, we loved the old man's stories. They were so rich, so deep, so involved, always interconnected and always about Carlisle. Then one day, just after your born, before your baptism, in fact, Mr. Cyning came up to us. Your mother was holding you in her arms. His eyes alighted on you and he smiled. 'Your boy will see like no other,' he said to us. 'He will see right into the deepest mysteries of Faërie, he will love the forest but it shall not be his home.' He said this as a kind of chant or benediction. Then he asked us, 'What have you decided to call him?' We told him Alfred and his smile widened, if that was at all possible. 'One who takes counsel with elves. Yes, that is a fitting name for a seer. He'll one day take over for me, I've no doubt.' With that he gave you a kiss and took his seat in the church. Well, you mother and I were confused, make no mistake, but two things were sure, Mr. Cyning loved you very much and if you could grow up at all to be like him, that would be a very good thing. All of that stuff about sight and Faërie made little sense to us, but we thought it meant something about being able to see wonder in the world around you. We even made Mr. Cyning your godfather, and let you play with him as often as we could.

"Then, as you grew up, you began to be scared all the time. You thought monsters were under your bed; you thought monsters were out in the forest. We didn't know what to do, but we thought Mr. Cyning's stories were scaring you. So we let you play with him a little less. One day you came home frightened and Mr. Cyning had a chat with me and then you. He said you needed to stop spending time with him altogether, for a while anyway. Then you started to watch more television and play on the computer and even when we encouraged you, you didn't want to spend as much time with in the forest. We just let it go. That was our mistake."

Alfred remembered back to his childhood. He could only just remember that he used to spend so much time with Mr. Cyning, that he had loved his stories. His time in Elfland had begun to remind him of those stories. "I remember," he said to his father. "It has been so long that I had nearly forgotten. Dad, the stories, I think they're all true. I've seen elves."

"I believe you," his father said. "Deep down your Mother and I knew Mr. Cyning was right. It began to dawn on us when we saw the shift in you after we got the television in the Inn. The change was so dramatic, that we knew there was something to Mr. Cyning's stories, that they had a kind of positive effect. You loved the forest less from that point on. But we soon learned beyond a doubt that Elfland was real."

"You did? When? How?"

"When you went off to university, your mother and I were working one evening when Mr. Cyning stopped by. We asked him if he had any stories. He said he did, but asked if we would kindly followed him. We left Philip in charge, it was a slow night, and followed Mr. Cyning. He took us out to his cottage on the edge of the forest. We went around the outside to his garden. There we saw something incredible. His whole garden was full of mushrooms, mushrooms of every shape and size. At the centre was a large one, too big to be real, nearly two feet it stood. Then, out of nowhere, we heard a voice. 'Have you brought them, sir?' it said. 'Yes,' replied Mr. Cyning, 'these are the boys parents.' The next thing I know, that mushroom in the centre is walking towards us, removing its cap to reveal a small brown mannish looking thing. 'Balthazar Toadstool, gnome and historian, at your service,' he said, doing a little bow. Jessica fainted and I went into a cold sweat. The old man told us about Elfland, Balthazar giving some of the history of Carlisle's interaction with it. Key to it all was a line of seers, usually born of different families, but always finding their way to the edges of Elfland. They told us you were such a seer. They knew there was little we could do to mend what had been done, but asked us to send you into the forest as often as we could. Balthazar seemed to know of your mother's cooking and suggested sending you in for mushrooms. For three years we sent you in as often as we could, but nothing ever happened. Not until this year."

"They were waiting. They knew something must be coming and waited until I could be of service," said Alfred.

"Yes, I think that's the way of things."

"Dad, we have to do something. The old woman I met told me to go back to the beginning and I'd find a way to stop the goblins."

"I know, Son. That's why I sent your mother to fetch Mr. Cyning. If what you say is true, then this village is about to see some trouble it's not seen for a very long time."

The two of them sat in silence. Alfred began to doze. The long walk seemed to have tired him out more than he realized. Not only that, but his chest and ribs began to aggravate him again. It seemed to him that the magic of the old woman's water was beginning wear. The room began to feel warm and close. Alfred could no longer keep his eyes open. His head fell against the back of the chair and he was asleep.

Alfred was beginning to recognize now when he entered a dream that allowed him to see things that were happening elsewhere. It took him a few moments, but he was able, eventually to recognize this dream for what it was. He looked around him and saw that he was in the forest. He wondered if perhaps he would see the elves, he was worried about them, especially after that attack. However, he saw nothing, not the feasting lights, nor any other sign of the elves. Instead he saw simply the trees and the forest floor. It was not long, however, before the sound of feet thumping through the forest. A voice that sounded more like a snarl said, "Pick up the pace, old man." Alfred looked on with horror as he saw Mr. Cyning being marched through the forest, his hands tied, by a couple of goblins. This, however, was all he saw for he was soon woken up by the entrance of his mother, who was concerned.

"I looked everywhere, George," she said, "but I can't find Mr. Cyning anywhere."

"That's because he's been taken," said Alfred.

"What do you mean?"

"I saw it, in a dream, he's been kidnapped by the goblins. We have to rescue him, I have to rescue him."

"What are you going to do, Son?" his father asked.

"I'll go to his cottage and look around. The old woman said to back to the beginning, well for all of us this began with Mr. Cyning."

"We'll go with you," his mother said.

"No," said his father. "I don't want you to get hurt, stay here. I'll go with Alf."

"No Dad, neither of you can come with me. I need to do this on my own. Besides, you need to stay here in Carlisle in case I fail and the goblins attack. Carlisle will need some people who can keep their heads, everyone else will be far too frightened."

"He's right, George," Jessica said, with a catch in her throat. "We have to let him do this on his own. If anyone can rescue Mr. Cyning, it will be you Alfred."

"Alright, but be careful," George said reluctantly.

"I will. You and Mom just stay safe and prepare to protect yourselves. Go to Mr. Cyning's house in a few hours. I'll leave a note telling you anything I've learned and where I'm going next."

With that Alfred was off to Mr. Cyning's house. His chest still twinged a bit, especially with his rucksack on his back, but he went on determinedly. When he arrived at the cottage he saw that it was a mess. Clearly it had been ransacked. Had not Mr. Cyning told him it was perilous to live so close to the border of Elfland? Now he could see why. There were no other homes around for miles, no one to hear the struggle or see what had happened.

Alfred tried to clean up. He saw books of myths and legends, tales of Arthurian legend, and a few private notes on Elfland among detritus. These last interested him most. He saw one labeled "Conversations with Balthazar" and another "Carlyle's Tale," but it was the one labeled "On the Dark Creatures of Elfland' that caught his eye. He flipped through the pages. He found references to will-o-the-wisps, boggarts, and then he saw one entitled "Concerning Goblins and Hobgoblins." He read:

> *There are no creatures in Elfland or the human world who are totally evil, though goblins are amongst the closest. There are many theories as to where the goblins come from, but what is sure is that they were once good. Whether they turned to evil the same time as man is uncertain. Being so very evil they cannot stand too much light. Fire bothers them unless it is used to hurt and destroy; the sun is nigh death to them; and even the moon at its fullest causes them to squint their eyes until nearly shut. Best avoided in dark tunnels, at which they could be adept should they take the time. Their hands are nimble and clever, but that cleverness*

is only ever put to wanton violence and destruction. Their teeth are usu-
ally razor sharp, and their hides tough, but not impenetrable. They can
be killed by any normal method, but it is best to avoid them altogether.

Occasionally, however, goblins come along who do not delight in
torture and destruction. They tend to be able to stay out even in a full
moon and will light fires to warm themselves. If these are allowed to
survive long enough, they tend to escape. There is a rumour that whole
tribes of good goblins, or hobgoblins as they tend to call themselves exist.
It is said that hobgoblins can vary from being only slightly better than
their goblin cousins to being positive forces for good. The rest tend to live
in neutrality, neither hating humans, elves, dwarves, etc., nor yet desir-
ing them good. The best can exist in full sunlight. However, the tales of
hobgoblins are few and it is doubted by many as to whether there are any
left, if there ever were any to begin with.

Goblins move in tribes led by. . . .

Here the text cut off. Nevertheless, Alfred was overjoyed, here at least
was some information on his foes. He tried to find the missing pages about
goblin government, again thinking this could be of use to him. He searched
to no effect. Still, this was something. He would remember to scribble a
note to his parents telling them about the goblins vulnerabilities. He looked
for anything on trolls or giants, but only found fairy tales and children's stories. Still, he took the time to read the shorter ones and put the longer ones
in his rucksack. If he had learned anything about Elfland and Mr. Cyning,
it was to trust in the truth telling abilities of stories.

"There must be more," Alfred said aloud. "Something I've missed,
something that will tell me where I need to go next." Then his eyes alighted
on a very old looking volume. Emblazoned on the side were the words
The History and Happenings of the Village of Carlisle: Interactions with the
Peoples of Faërie. Alfred leafed through the pages and came across an entry
from over a millennium ago.

Our annals record that once during the reign of King Alfred the
Great in the southern lands of our island, the goblins, vile, nasty, evil
creatures that they are, besieged the village. A certain person, be he faerie
or human it is not recorded, named Alvin, collected the citizens in St.
Nicholas's Church. The goblins attempted to set fire to the church, but
it was too well made. Eventually, they broke down the doors and found
the church empty. Enraged, the goblins began to tear apart the inside
of the church. They were drawn out, however, by voices from without.

The village people surrounded them, having lit torches for protection and armed themselves. It seems that Alvin knew of a secret passageway from the church to somewhere in the forest

A battle then began that shall not be soon forgot. Goblins, humans, and faeries, as well as other creatures of Faërie unknown to us, some small, brown and leathery, others, were short and heavily bearded, lay dead in the streets of Carlisle and still the battle raged on. It was not until the Faërie Queen herself arrived and with her the rising of the sun that goblins and other foul creatures of Faërie were driven off. A pact was then made with the Faërie Queen that the position of here there was a smudge which made the word illegible *would be held by a human in Carlisle to remind the people both of their own great victory and the part the people of Faërie played in it as well.*

"This is it!" exclaimed Alfred. "I have to find this secret passage in the basement of the church." Alfred quickly scribbled another note to his parents about going to find the secret passage. He deliberated for a moment as to whether or not he should leave the book for them, but decided to take it. "Better I have it than the goblins come back, find it, and destroy it. Alfred's rucksack was now considerably heavier and his chest hurt even more. Huffing and puffing, he shouldered the pack and made his way back into town.

Alfred longed to put on his elvin garments and sword, he thought they might lessen the weight on his back. But no, he reasoned with himself, if the people of Carlisle saw him dressed in what they would assume is fancy dress, he would never get to the church, let alone in it. So on he trudged, wincing at the pain in his chest and adjusting the straps of his rucksack as often as he could.

The church of St. Nicholas was one of those few churches into which a person could go at almost any hour during the day. Locked boxes were set up all around the inside to take donations and there were plenty of places to sit quietly. When Alfred went in, he saw no one else. The light shone through the stained-glass windows, but Alfred had little time to notice the beauty of the church.

He began to search around, looking for a secret passageway, but nothing presented itself. He looked for over an hour, the pain in his chest increasing every moment. "Damnit!" he whispered loudly. "Where is the entrance?" He sat in a huff near one of the more decorative windows. He looked out it, wondering if it had been in place when the goblins had attacked. As he looked at it, he finally began to notice it. It was a triumphant battle scene. Perhaps it had been meant to depict Christ's conquering at the second coming, but it looked much like what the book had described as the battle around the church. The demons and imps looked remarkably like the goblins he had seen. Even the angels reminded him of the elves. He stared long at one in particular until he realized, "That has to be Carlyle." As he said the words, a stone in the floor near the font next to him began to move. He looked down. There was a ladder. This must be the secret passage.

Alfred set his rucksack over the man-sized whole that had opened in the floor. He pulled out his Elfland attire and quickly changed. He left his normal clothes in a pew. He the girded his sword about him, slung his pack on his shoulders, winced in pain, and descended into the hole.

It was too dark for him to see. "I should have brought a torch," he whispered to himself. He continued down the ladder and came to solid ground. He turned round to face front, took a step, and fell down what felt like a dozen stairs. The pain in his chest was becoming unbearable, but he got to his feet. He felt gingerly in front of him with feet; more stairs. He did not know how far down these stairs went, but he traveled on. He fell twice more before he came to a long stretch of flat surface. The ground and walls around him were earthy at first, but as he walked on they turned more to stone.

Doubts and fears began to creep upon him in the dark. What if he didn't get to the forest in time? What if the goblins attacked before he could find help? Who did he think he was, anyway? As if he could do anything against such forces of evil. Alfred stopped, his chest burned with pain, sweat was pouring from his face. The weight of his rucksack seemed to have increased with every step he took. Yes, that's it. Just stop, the doubts said to him. There's nothing more you can do. You're just a lazy boy who thought himself a man. You're too weak, too young. The tunnel seemed to be getting warmer, everything began to swim before Alfred's eyes. He began to doze.

In that place between sleep and wake, Alfred began to remember his old dreams. He remembered the song of the elves. He remembered his battle against the giant. He remembered his conversations with Mr. Cyning. It was never about him, who he was or how special he was. There was nothing special about him, but that did not matter. What mattered was only to do what he had been tasked. Alfred struggled forward.

Neither the pain in his chest, nor the temptations ceased, but he plodded onward. He thought he saw a light in the distance, but before he could reach it he stumbled into something. "Arghh," said a voice in the dark. "And what have we here, a wayward elf I would say, a wounded one. All the worse for you." With that, Alfred was attacked.

Alfred recognized the creature for a goblin and drew his sword. It felt heavy in his hand. "Come on then!" he shouted, sounding braver than he felt, but just as tired. The goblin lunged with a sword of its own, but Alfred deflected its thrust. It came at him again, this time its sword point going home into Alfred's shoulder. It then sliced him against his already painful chest. This would have been the death blow had Alfred not begun to jump back already. Then Alfred lunged with his sword shouting, "I wounded the terrible giant. I have slain attacking goblins. You will not stand before me." He brought his blade crashing down on the goblins head. It fell to the ground, dead. Alfred picked up his sword, took two steps, and fell to the ground next to it.

Chapter 8

Alfred began to hear voices around him. The voices sounded deep and rough and old. They spoke English, but it sounded odd, as if their tongues were made to speak something much older. "Who is he?" said one of the voices.

"He's not one of the ilfa, though he's dressed and armed by them. You can tell that by looking at him," said another.

"He must be a mortal and is likely the Seer our Lady told us of," said a voice which sounded as if it were made of ancient stone.

"He killed one of the goblins, whoever he is, and for that he has my thanks," said another voice.

"My name is Alfred Perkins. I am the Seer and I have slain many goblins and wounded a giant. I have come to help Elfland in its time of need and to defend my own village of Carlisle, with my life if necessary. Declare yourselves now, are you friends or enemies." Alfred feebly reached for his sword. Where this courage came from, he was not sure.

"Careful with that, my child," said the old voice. "We dweorgas are no friends of the nihtgengan, though we tend to keep to ourselves."

"Dwarves!" he exclaimed as he looked around himself. His vision finally refocused he noticed that all around him were people no taller than four feet, most shorter. All varying shades of a rather ruddy complexion with beards thick and braided dangling down to their knees. Most wore leather jerkins, many chain-mail.

"Yes, I believe that is what you mortals call us now," said the old voice again. "We are the Hamorlingas, at your service, Master Seer."

"Alfred Perkins, at yours," he said getting to his feet and attempting a bow. He began to fall forward.

"Careful now, Master Seer," said a dwarf standing near him and catching him as he began to fall. "You're still not fully recovered. Not yet."

"Tell me," said Alfred sitting back down on the stone bed he had been lying on, "what happened? How did I end up here? The last thing I remember was fighting that goblin."

"Well, you killed him, and no mistake," said the dwarf who caught him. "Then I found you while searching for one of our brothers who went missing a few days ago. You were nigh death for sure, if it weren't for our king, Lord Hrothmor, you surely would be dead."

"Well then I am much obliged to you and perhaps can be of help as well. I have seen a vision of your missing brother."

"You have?" said the elder dwarf.

"Yes, my Lord," said Alfred, guessing the ancient dwarf before him was the king. "He was somewhere deep in the mountain, being tortured by the goblins."

"Adelbert," said Hrothmor to the dwarf near Alfred, "put together a small company go down deep, perhaps they work in the forgotten mines, quickly, there is no time to lose."

"Please, my Lord, allow me to accompany them," said Alfred as Adelbert began to make preparations.

"No, Master Seer. I cannot allow that. You are still too weak from your wounds. You must rest. There will be time enough for heroic deeds. Now, Hamorlingas, to arms. Find our brother. If he be dead, avenge him, if alive bring him back quickly and leave the goblins for another time. Go forth, to honour to victory."

With that Alfred was left alone in the room with just one other dwarf who had been present, but not chosen for the mission. He was, it seemed, smaller than the other dwarves. His fingers looked stained black and from his belt, beneath his beard, Alfred thought he spied quills and a small clay bottle he assumed held ink. Alfred noticed the room did hold a few bookshelves, amongst the many shelves of weaponry and blacksmithing tools. The dwarves, Alfred guessed, were not generally bookish people.

"Is there anyway I may be of service to you Master dwarf," Alfred said to the lone dwarf.

"Well," he replied, "I noticed in your bag a few books and papers, would you mind if I looked at them. I want to see if we should have copies for our library, it is, after all, not large."

"By all means," Alfred replied. "May I ask your name?"

"Bócrædere, is my name, keeper of this poor excuse for a Scriptorium and library. Please, feel free to peruse any of our works. We do not write much, though we have many tales to tell. Whenever our bard sings, I try to take notes to write what I hear later."

Alfred looked through the leathery tomes on the shelves, *Rodortungol and the Bear*, *Ælfandwlita the Fair*, *Afolbóg and the Eoten*. "Are these the tales of your people, the Hamorlingas?" Alfred asked.

"Some yes," replied Bócrædere. Afolbóg is my father and Rodortungol is nephew to the king. Ælfandwlita, however, is more likely a folk tale. He's said to have been the child of a dwarf and an elf. His is a story of love. He loved a mortal, whose name we have long since forgotten. In the story he simply calls her Ælfscíene, Beautiful as an Elf. It is a sad tale. We do not often tell it, except when we want to feel sorrowful."

"Why would you want to feel sorrowful?"

"It is good for the dwarves to feel sorrow. We are a hardy people, prone to working hard and long, to loving work and battle for their own sake. The stories of sorrow remind us to love beauty, to love goodness. Without them we would lose ourselves in work and battle. It is why we keep training dwarves to be bards. It is why my own position exists, without us the dwarves would be little better than crafty creatures."

Alfred sat pondering what he had just heard while handing over the texts he had brought with him to Bócrædere. His chest still bothered him and his head began to swim, he laid back down on the stone table he had awoken on and fell asleep.

Alfred began to see a vision in his sleep. This time he had no doubts that what he saw was a vision. He was back in the bottom of the cave where he had previously seen the dwarf being tortured. The room was much darker, the great fire built up to torture the dwarf had been allowed to burn low. Alfred thought it must be because the goblins cannot stand the light of fire when it is used for any purpose other than destruction.

There were a few goblins still around, most of them sleeping, though two stood guard over something, though Alfred could not quite see what. He moved closer, being unobserved by the goblins, and saw a pitiful sight. There between the two armed goblins, sat a dwarf, badly injured, its beard almost entirely plucked out, the hair on its head burnt, like its skin, to a crisp. Alfred heard a noise behind him, quietly, but quickly, the dwarves were making their way into the cavern. Their chain-mail only lightly clinking, they slew the first two sleeping goblins they came to. Their noise in doing so, however, woke the other goblins.

Now they had a battle on their hands, and Alfred was very much afraid they would be overwhelmed. Alfred had not, however, given thought to the hardiness of the dwarves. Wielding mattocks, pickaxes, and battle axes, they stormed the wakening goblins. The goblins soon overcame their dreariness and the battle was even. Alfred tried to see what had become of the captured dwarf, but could see nothing, at first. As he moved closer to the spot where he was held prisoner he saw the two goblin guards lying dead and the dwarf, his hands bound and body injured, taking one of their daggers, freeing himself from his bonds and making his way towards the fray. "To me, Hamorlingas!" he shouted. The dwarves rallied and Alfred woke up.

He looked around in the Scriptorium and found Bócrædere speaking in hushed tones with King Hrothmor. "They've found the lost dwarf," Alfred told them, "and are battling the goblins now."

"Quick, Bócrædere, gather another group of dwarves and find our brothers, aid them in this battle and hurry them home."

"Yes, my king," and with that, Bócrædere ran from the room.

"You have my thanks, Master Seer," said the king.

"I merely do what I was meant to," replied Alfred.

"Ah, but you do not have to. Think, you could have these visions and disbelieve them, or keep them to yourself. Yet you would still be a seer. By sharing them you go beyond what is merely natural to you."

"My Lord, what will you do concerning the goblins? How will you stop them, for if they are not stopped, my home and the homes of all those in Carlisle will be destroyed? Not only them, but your own halls will likely be overrun."

"That I know full well, Master Seer. But as for what is to be done, I cannot say for certain. We dwarves are a warrior people and will fight the horrid nihtgengan to be certain, but we cannot, I think, defeat them. We are now too few, and they have clearly been breeding in their time away from us. No, we cannot go on the attack, we must shore up our defences."

"My Lord, is not there not honour in battle, even in defeat?"

"Yes, Master Seer, but we dwarves are too few to value honour over life in these later times. Centuries ago we would have gone on the attack. Ah, you would have seen something then. My grandfather was king, Hamorwealden, the dwarven armies he commanded were a sight to be seen. Each dwarf a warrior and a poet, capable of singing their own lays of their glorious deeds after a battle. He aided in the defence of Carlisle in a way I wish I could. We are a fallen people. Our skill in mining, smithing, and léoþcræft all are lesser than in the days of grandsires."

Before Alfred could again respond the two troops of dwarves King Hrothmor had sent into the roots of the mountains returned. All of them looked wounded, two were being carried, lifeless. Alfred looked for both Bócrædere and the captured dwarf. Relieved he saw them both towards the front. "I am sorry Master Seer, but as the Scriptorium doubles as our infirmary, I must ask you to give up your bed for the wounded among us, several dwarves can lie where you sit," Bócrædere said to him leading the liberated dwarf to the bed.

"Of course," replied Alfred, hopping down. His chest was beginning to bother him a little less. "I must be going anyway, I must find the elves if I am to save Carlisle."

"The elves?" said the injured dwarf. "Can you not find aid from amongst the dwarves? We may be small to your eyes, but we are hardy folk."

"That I know, for I have seen you at battle in a vision," replied Alfred, "but I will not go against the wishes of your king."

"What is this I hear, brother?" said the injured dwarf to the king. "Are we not to battle these infernal nihtgengan with the humans and elves as we did in the days of our fathers and grandfathers?"

"No, Hamorson, we are not. You know as well as that were we to go to battle, even if our warriors survived, the goblins would ascend our mountain and kill those left behind."

"You forget the strength of our women, and even our children. They are more than enough for the nihtgengan that would be left behind."

"And you forget that they fight not alone. I have had word, as you well know for it is what sent you misguidedly looking for them in the first place, that eotenas and trolls have joined forces with the nihtgengan. Our people would be destroyed. We cannot think only of honour and valour, we must defend ourselves. The dwarves must first be for the dwarves."

It was then that Alfred remembered what had sent him into the tunnels under the church. "Mr. Cyning!" he exclaimed.

"What about him, Master Seer?" asked Hamorson.

"The goblins have captured him. That fight with the goblin must have driven it from my memory. I have to find him."

"Are you sure?" asked Hamorson worriedly.

"I saw it in a vision. When I went to his cottage it had been ransacked and he was gone. Please, King Hrothmor, you must help me find him. I understand if you think you must defend your people rather than go to war, though I may disagree, but you must help me rescue Mr. Cyning. Men are not so hardy as dwarves and that is when they are young. Mr. Cyning is quite old now and will not suffer torture long."

"We have already lost two of our own people rescuing one of our own. I am afraid I cannot risk more, even for one so connected with our realm as Oliver Cyning."

"Brother, you cannot be serious. There is a man, like as not in our own mountain somewhere far below who needs our help. Need I remind you who Oliver Cyning is? The importance of him? Why he is—"

"I know very well who he is and what he stands for brother. Do not forget your place. We must protect ourselves; if we go in search of this man there will be no dwarves left as I foresee."

"Hammer and tongs, brother! You have become nearsighted indeed if you cannot see that what happens beyond our borders affects us as well. We must help the Seer."

"Enough! Do not forget your place. I am king, I am the giver of gifts, I am lord and father in this mountain. I will let no more of my people go in search of the goblins. We will block of the tunnels leading to the cavern where you were kept. Tonight we shall feast in the meed-hall and send off our fallen brothers and welcome back my brother." With that, the king stormed out of the room. Alfred was stunned, uncertain of what to do next. He stood in a daze while the dwarves bustled about around him.

"Come, Master Seer," said Bócrædere, "the King has asked me to prepare a room for you. You are to join us tonight at the feast and then tomorrow will be escorted to the edge of our kingdom to go where you will. I am sorry about Oliver Cyning, he told me many of my favourite non-dwarven stories, many years ago." Alfred followed listlessly. Bócrædere showed Alfred to his room, he had to duck in order to enter, but the ceiling inside went up further than he could see. He vaguely heard Bócrædere say something about fire and flues. Alfred sat down on the bed. "I will return to you when it is time for the feast," Bócrædere made a bow and left the room. Alfred fell asleep.

Alfred's visions were coming more frequently to him. He wondered if it was the prolonged exposure to Elfland. His chest was almost completely healed, thanks in part to the cares of the dwarves, but Alfred thought simply the air invigorated him as well. Alfred's vision placed him somewhere in the forest. He saw two monstrous creatures, much larger than elves or humans, but smaller, at least, than the giant he had faced. Their hides were grey and it almost looked as though chunks of their flesh was missing. Alfred assumed these were trolls. He worried about having to face them. It seemed to him that swords would have little effect on skin so stony in appearance. They walked single file, each carrying a large chain. Between them, at the centre of the chain stood a person. At first, Alfred did not recognize him, but as his vision became clearer, he noticed that the man had a striking resemblance to Mr. Cyning. Only now Mr. Cyning was dressed, as Alfred reminded himself he was as well, in the raiment of the elves. He did not look injured. He kept talking to the trolls. "Take your time, my rocky friends, morning is coming and you shall soon find your path."

"Quiet, maggot!" shouted the troll behind him.

"Don't let him inside your head," said the other. "Just keeping walking, we'll get him to our cave before sunrise."

"You're lucky," said the first troll to Mr. Cyning. "If we weren't under orders, we'd split you in two and share you between us."

"Who would have heads, and who tails? There's more meat at the top, unless you have more interest in legs. Surely you," Mr. Cyning addressed the troll behind him, "will have second choice. You are clearly not the leader. No, I suppose your compatriot in front would have first choice, if choice there were."

The troll behind Mr. Cyning would perhaps have eaten him whole if he had not been checked by the troll in front. "Quiet!" he hissed. "We'll wake up the whole forest and bring all the elves and dwarves and who knows what else down on us." As they waited, Alfred noticed a small ring of mushrooms nearby, one of them quite over large. "Balthazar," he said excitedly. At least now he knew that Mr. Cyning was not alone, and seemingly unharmed. Though he shuddered to think what would happen to him if he remained in the company of trolls.

Chapter 9

When Bócrædere came to take Alfred to the feast, Alfred was well rested and feeling better about the fate of Mr. Cyning. He confided in Bócrædere about his vision. "Well, it's a relief to know he's safe," Bócrædere said as he led Alfred to a staircase which they began to ascend. "And you are quite sure, Master Seer, that they were in the forest and not the mountain?"

"Yes, the trolls were considerably worried about being caught out in sunlight. Does it hurt them like it does goblins?"

"Worse, if stories are to be believed. According to all our lays, trolls will revert to the stone from which they are made if they continue in the sunlight."

"Really? Why? I mean, how are they made from stone?"

"Well, there are certainly many theories as to the origins of the trolls. One of our stories—" Bócrædere stopped.

"Bringing the Seer to the feast, Bócrædere?"

"Indeed I am, Hamorson. Should you not also be there? It is, after all, in your honour as well as those of our fallen brothers."

"If it were not for the fallen I would not go at all. My cowardly brother hiding behind the pretences of protecting our people when he knows we must fight the nihtgengan if we desire to be safe.

"Come, Master Seer, walk with me a moment. Tell them we are coming presently, Bócrædere."

"As you wish." Bócrædere ran up the stairs and Alfred stood alongside Hamorson. Alfred told him of his vision.

"Aye that is good news, or at least better than we feared. And you say he did not look injured."

"No, he was in perfect health, aside from being chained between two trolls."

"Oliver Cyning can certainly hold his own against a couple of dim-witted trolls, even if one of them did seem to have half a brain. Trust me, Master Seer, when we get into the forest, I would not be surprised if found him sitting patiently between two troll statues."

"When we go to the forest? I thought the king commanded all dwarves to stay and protect the mountain."

"My brother has forgotten what it means to be king. No, Master Seer, there are a few of us amongst the dwarves who will go with you to defeat the nihtgengan."

Alfred was happy to know he would not be going alone from the mountain, but concerned how the king would react to this defiance. Still, Alfred and Hamorson climbed the remainder of the stairs and Alfred noticed that they were now outside. He would have been quite cold, but there were numerous fires burning. Alfred looked up and saw what looked like more mountain.

"That's right, Master Seer," Hamorson turned to see Alfred staring up and around, "our meed hall is carved out of the very top of the mountain. We may be smithies and miners, but we love the world around us, especially the night sky."

"This is stunning," said Alfred, "but how do we never see you feasting on the mountain from Carlisle?"

"Need you ask? Have you not spent enough time here to realize that you do not see what do you not look at properly. You humans work so hard to convince yourselves that we are naught but myths and legends, it is little wonder you do not see us even atop the mountain at such a great distance. Though we have celebrated little of late, so it is certainly no wonder you have never noticed. This is our first celebration in over a century."

The two of them walked to a table, where large bowls, even large to Alfred, were filled with mead. Alfred could smell the roasting of a boar from one of the nearby fires. The king stood before them all and called his brother as well as the families of the two fallen dwarves to him at the head of the mead hall. To his brother he gave a large hammer, too large for smithing, Alfred thought to himself. It must have either been ceremonial or perhaps for battle. Alfred could see two weeping female dwarves and their children receiving gold and gems from the king's dweorgild he thought he heard the king say. Suddenly he heard the King calling his own name.

"Come Master Seer, Alfred Perkins, you too are to be rewarded. If it were not for your visions my brother would be lost to us and the nihtgengan may have found their way into our halls. Therefore I present you mail crafted by my people for you, may it turn back the blades of the accursed in the future. We also present you with this shield, once made for a different human, and now given to you." On the shield was a red, rampant unicorn.

"Thank you King Hrothmor. May these find use in battle soon," Alfred bowed to the king. Hrothmor looked briefly disgruntled at Alfred's words, but as there was a general cheer from the dwarves, he said nothing.

There was a call for a song and a small troop of dwarves came to the fore, several with instruments. The one in front Alfred presumed to be the bard. But Alfred could not hear the song, he was greeted by every dwarf as he went back to his seat, being offered deep pulls from their mead bowls. The song, nevertheless, left an impact on Alfred's heart. It made him feel ready for battle, but also made him feel the sorrow that comes from a world that needs battle at all. His head began to swim and he asked to be directed back to his room. Who guided him, he could not say, but eventually he returned to his room. Alfred's head hit the pillow and he knew no more until morning.

A dwarf woman who introduced herself as Magda, woke him in the morning. She led him to an internal mess hall where he breakfasted with the warriors of King Hrothmor. Hamorson was sitting at one end of the long table with two other dwarves and beckoned for Magda to lead him there. Alfred joined the dwarves and found himself in a war counsel. "I have been told both of your battle with the goblin in our halls and your desire to join the party in search of me," said Hamorson. "I must say, Master Seer, I am even more hopeful of our venture to rescue Oliver Cyning that I was yesterday. We must sneak away, just the four of us."

Alfred looked at the other two dwarves, realising that one of them was Bócrædere and the other reintroduced himself as Adelbert, the dwarf Hrothmor sent in the first instance to seek after Hamorson. Alfred repeated again his vision of Mr. Cyning in the forest with the trolls. Then Alfred asked "How are we to leave? The King has declared that all his people are to remain here in order to defend his kingdom."

"My brother has asked for a small troop to search the corridor where you were found for any other nihtgengan before it is blocked up by some of our more skilled miners. We will volunteer to search and you can say you are desiring to return home to defend your own people. He will not be able to refuse if we ask in a public manner. Then we will take one of the side tunnels which leads to the forest. From there we will try to gather news from the gnomes or fairies."

All assented to the plan and then ate in silence. Alfred returned to his room to pack his things. Bócrædere came bringing the books and papers Alfred had leant him. "We're all ready. Hamorson has already been to see the king, who did not refuse his request. Do you have all your things ready?"

"Nearly," Alfred replied. "I simply need to put on this mail the king gave me." Alfred finished dressing and he and Bócrædere both set off down the tunnels to where the dwarven mines intersected with this ancient tunnel to Carlisle. When they arrived, the King was there waiting for them.

"Master Seer, we owe you a great debt, and while I can send no one with you to combat the evil that is already on our own doorstep, I wish to give you aids in the combat. Here is a scabbard for your sword. The jewels were worked into it by some of our best craftsdwarves from ages past. It will fit any sword, and sharpens your blade both when you sheathe and unsheathe it."

Alfred bowed and accepted the gift. "I also give to you this dwarven made battle-axe. It was once made for a different man many centuries ago." Alfred took the axe and examined it. It was enormous, but not unwieldy; it was completely green. "Go in peace, Alfred George's son, Master Seer. May the hair on your face never fall out. Know that my good will goes with you in your endeavours. I now commit into the hands of these three (pointing to Hamorson, Adelbert, and Bócrædere) to see you safely into the tunnels." With that the king and his coterie began their return to the king's halls while the miners continued to work on blocking the very passage Alfred was now to take.

The troop soon left behind all the miners and Alfred began to recognize the place where he had battled with the goblin. "Who made this tunnel," Alfred asked.

"No one knows for sure," Bócrædere replied. "It has existed for over a thousand years, that we know for sure, and was often used to allow communication between all of Elfland and Carlisle."

"It seems now, however, as though it might allow communication between nothing at best or the nihtgengan and Carlisle at worst," said Hamorson.

Alfred had not thought of this, but it was quite true. What if the goblins, discovering they could not access the mountain kingdom of the dwarves, realized that the tunnel led into Carlisle?

"Torches out, lads," said Adelbert. "It's going to get too dark even for the dwarves, let alone Master Seer." Adelbert handed Alfred a torch and lit it from a flint he kept on him while Bócrædere and Hamorson pulled torches from their own packs. The group turned a corner before reaching the church and plunged into darkness.

Were it not for their torches Alfred is sure he would have been lost forever. As they walked on he continually noticed openings in the walls. Some of which, Adelbert told him, led back to the main tunnels and others which led to an underground maze created by water from the lake and river.

They walked for hours. At one point, perhaps hearing Alfred's stomach rumble, Adelbert reached into his pack and handed Alfred some cured meat. It nearly broke Alfred's teeth at first, being made for dwarven maws which are sturdier than humans'. It softened after a bit and Alfred's hunger was sated. More time went by and finally, though Alfred thought he was imagining it, the path began to climb. There was a light ahead.

They extinguished their torches and exited the tunnel. They were in the forest, quite far from the Mountain, but not too far from the village. Alfred thought he recognized some of the trees. There was no time, however to relax. Adelbert hissed at them to be quiet and take cover. Moments later Alfred heard the rustling of leaves, indicative of a large group moving through the undergrowth. Despite an early start, the sun was already beginning to set, and the forest here was particularly dense, only a few misguided rays were still finding their way to the forest floor. Alfred soon recognized one of the voices and then the other, he ran out to meet them, the dwarves attempting to stop him.

"Balthazar, Carlyle, how do you come to be here?" he exclaimed. Before him stood, equally awe-struck, the gnome, Carlyle the elf, and a female elf unknown to Alfred. All were dressed for battle. Even little Balthazar had on him a short dagger, which made a rather long sword in his small brown hands.

The shock, however, ended quickly as Carlyle and Alfred embraced. Balthazar made a bow to him and even the she-elf recognized Alfred. He had not realized it at the time, but she was the elf warrior who stood beside him when the giant attacked. Alfred looked at her now. Like all her race she was stunningly beautiful. Her hair was raven, her cheeks roses, her eyes a misty sea in a fog. Alfred made a bow to her and asked the name of such a valiant warrior.

"I am Lucinda, fair Seer," she said in reply. "It is an honour to work and fight alongside such a valiant mortal. It has been long since Lord Carlyle and I have had the opportunity."

"Right you are, my wife," chimed in Carlyle. "Before long, I foresee that our Seer will be worthy not only of his name Alfred but of Rædælf as well, for we shall take counsel from him, else I see not well."

"Nay husband, I believe you to be right. It is also on my heart that we shall seek his counsel. In truth, we seek it now, for we have lost the path.

"But we have been rude, husband, and have not greeted the dweorgas. These valiant ones have seen battle as well, it is written on their faces."

Carlyle looked gravely at Lucinda, "Too right you are. Come friends and brothers, we are Carlyle and Lucinda. Tell us your names and your adventures."

The dwarves, with occasional interruptions from Alfred, introduced themselves and told their tale. "I am sorry about your brother, Hamorson. I pray he may not have great cause to regret his decisions as things will not go well for your people if he does."

"I fear you are right," Hamorson replied. "All the more reason we must find Oliver Cyning, and then work towards defeating those terrible niht-gengan. The Seer has told us they also have giants and trolls with them, have you encountered any of them?"

"Only the giant have we encountered," Lucinda looked at Alfred as she said this. "This is the first we have heard of their use of trolls. If true, then the six of us may not be enough."

"There are seven of us here, my Lady. Pray do not forget that we gnomes can fight as well as give wisdom," chimed Balthazar.

"Indeed, I have not forgotten it. However, the people of Carlisle must be prepared, therefore I recommend we send you to the Seer's parents. Constant watch must be put on the church, else the goblins may attack the peoples unawares. We must keep the Seer with us and you alone can reach the village without attracting too much attention."

"Of course my Lady. I should have thought of that myself. I will go off at once. I will also send word throughout the forest. Perhaps the other inhabitants of Elfland will be able to help." With that, Balthazar wriggled himself into the ground and disappeared like a fish beneath water.

Chapter 10

Alfred, the dwarves, and the elves sat down to discuss what to do next. "We must begin to search the forest for signs of trolls," said Adelbert. "Nonsense, they'll be long underground. I say we begin drumming up what help we can. I trust in my strength and the strength of all dwarves, but three dwarves, two elves, and a human will have little to do against an army of goblins, trolls, and giants," said Hamorson.

"I agree with Hamorson. Come Lady, let us find our scattered people. They may have returned to the castle. We will put together an army to fight these wicked beasts," replied Carlyle.

"We're losing time," said Alfred. "Who knows what's happened to Mr. Cyning? We have to save him."

The four of them continued to argue the merits of their plans when the Lady Lucinda lifted her hand. "Hold," she said. She did not shout, she spoke barely above a whisper, but there was force behind her voice. They stopped arguing. "What do think Master Librarian?" she asked of Bócrædere.

"Well, madam, it seems to me that what we need most is information. There are two ways of gathering it. We could ask for help from the other creatures in the forest, or—"

"Yes?"

"Or we could have the Seer seek for answers in his dreams."

"I agree with our learnéd dwarf friend," the Lady announced to all present. "I think it right for our Seer to look for news. In the mean time, I will seek what creatures of the wood that may be nearby. I am sure some fairies, or perhaps even some gnomes may be found."

"Wait," said Alfred. The Lady stopped and all eyes turned toward him. The sun was beginning to set. "I have no control over what I see. Sometimes I see things and other times not."

"Yet you must try," Lucinda replied. "Our fates rest with you, now you must rest with fate. Sleep with an aim to seeing." With that Lucinda went searching amongst the trees, humming to herself.

"She is surely right," Carlyle said. "Come, my friends, let us make camp here so our Seer may sleep and we may guard him."

Alfred resigned himself to his fate. He would sleep now and try to see. He was already capable of recognising dream from vision, perhaps he was ready to invoke a vision. The dwarves got a fire going and Carlyle added something to it. The smoke went an almost ruddy color and there was a scent of roses in the air. "These scents may aid you, both in sleep and in seeing," he said in answer to Alfred's quizzical look.

Alfred laid his head on his pack as the warmth and scents of the rose fire carried him off to sleep. Alfred began to see something, but was not sure at first if it were a dream or a vision. There were roses everywhere, which made him think it a dream, but the scene soon changed. He found himself inside a shallow cave. It was part dirt and part rock. Alfred could see the sun setting through the mouth of the cave, near which was standing a goblin, squinting its eyes. "Wake up, maggots," it shouted. "That accursed sun is almost down, soon it will be safe for trolls and goblins." Alfred looked to see to whom the goblin was speaking. At the back of the cave he saw several goblins curled up and two large trolls, between them was changed Mr. Cyning.

"Oh please," said Mr. Cyning, "don't get up on my account, lads. Feel free to sleep the night away and wait until tomorrow morning to make your start." He laughed, but it was clear that was pain in his breathing. He was covered in cuts and bruises.

"Quiet you," shouted the goblin at the mouth of the cave. "Get up you good-for-nothings! We have to get him back to camp. King Catseyes expected us back yesterday. He so wants this prisoner. It's too bad, really, we could have some fun." The goblin aimed a kick at Mr. Cyning, who moved, almost lazily, out of the way causing the goblin to strike one of the trolls. The troll felt nothing, but the goblin began howling in pain.

"It's best not to strike trolls, but sunlight or moonlight," said Mr. Cyning quietly. Rather than respond, the goblin simply leered at him as it shook the trolls awake. Alfred watched them pack up and begin heading out. He looked for any signs that could indicate where they were in the forest, what direction they were headed in, anything. Along the side of the hill wherein the goblins and trolls had taken refuge from the sun, blossomed many wildflowers. A light seemed to come from them as the evil creatures left. While the light lacked a distinct color, it seemed to him to be seething, as if in anger over what had recently occupied it. Alfred thought the creatures were leading Mr. Cyning to the South, but where the South headed he could not tell.

Alfred yawned and opened his eyes. "What news, Master Seer?" asked Hamorson loudly. The group gathered around Alfred and it dawned on him what a strange company they make: Two very battle weary dwarves and one bookish one who still carried ink pots and quills on his belt alongside his mattock and axe, and two elves almost too beautiful to behold. He sat up and saw the sun rising. He knew the creatures must take refuge and so without leaving out a single aspect, he told them of his dream.

"They slept in a fairy-mound?" exclaimed Adelbert. "The fairies won't take too kindly to that. I'm surprised they discovered no mischief when they departed."

Alfred suddenly remembered the stories about men disappearing atop hills, often with fairy-rings at the top. He remembered Mr. Cyning once telling him the story of Robert Kirk. "I thought elves lived in fairy-mounds," he said at last

"No, Seer," replied Carlyle. "We build like men, in fact we taught them to build, but we taught them to work with nature, not against it. Most of the elves live in and around the Faërie Queen's Castle away north."

Alfred had no time to ask how humans had never found this castle, however, as Lucinda had just come back from speaking to a tree, or so it seemed. "I have just spoken with one of the fairies," she said to the group. "She believes she knows which mound Alfred saw. She is willing to guide us."

A small beam of light hit Alfred in the eye. It was so strong he thought he had gone blind. The light dulled, however, and when he looked again he saw a tiny person, much smaller than Balthazar, perhaps no more than six inches tall. She was intensely white, with hints of yellow throughout. "Siofra Rowan, at your service," the fairy said, doing a mid-air curtsey.

The group trudged on, following the white light of the fairy. In her presence, Alfred saw an extra beauty in the forest. He understood at last why it was called Fey Forest. In her light the forest indeed seemed fey, wild and yet beautiful beyond compare. Not only had the fairy-light helped the Seer to see even more clearly the beauty of the forest, he began to see all manner of creatures before unnoticed by him. In every collection of mushrooms he saw their gnome shepherd clearly; behind every flower and tree he saw the fairies hiding from the racket made by the dwarves. They too seemed moved to see more clearly in the fairy-light. Bócrædere in particular seemed moved to tears at the beauty of the wood. The beauty switched to that fey wildness in an instant, however, as they approached the cave Alfred saw in his vision.

"Is this the cave, dear mortal?" asked the fairy.

"It is indeed, Lady Rowan," Alfred replied.

"Then I shall just nip in and have a chat with my cousins. We fairies are generally none too trusting of you big folk, even if you are with them your ladyship," she said making a curtsey to Lucinda. She flew off to the fairy mound and went inside. Adelbert, meanwhile, looked nervous, fingering the blade of his axe with one hand and stroking his beard with the other.

Adelbert noticed Alfred staring at him, "These fairies make me nervous. Their mischievous at the best of times. They don't take too kindly to dwarves, but we need the wood for our forges. Anyway, even a friendly fairy might play you a trick as a joke. The ones who live here are livid, I can feel it in the air, in the ground beneath my feet. They mean to do something worse than mischief, and I for one don't want to be on the wrong side of it."

"It'll be good to have them on our side for once, all the same," said Hamorson.

"If they are on our side," retorted Adelbert.

"Why wouldn't they be?" asked Alfred.

"Fairies keep to themselves. You heard Siofra," said Hamorson, "even with Carlyle and Lucinda, elvin royalty, they aren't going to trust us to be on their side. Fairies protect the things that grow. They have a special relationship with trees and flowers particularly. They're like gnomes, they shepherd, they garden all of nature. They tend not to mind elves, but aren't especially allied to them, they obey the Queen, but they also have their own. Dwarves and humans they generally dislike, those as don't find us simply comical. One thing's for sure, though, they hate the evil things more than any disdain they could have for us. They must be right livid that a group of goblins and trolls camped in their mound."

Siofra seemed to be gone for quite a long time. The time ticked by, Alfred tried to watch out for the fairies. They were harder to see without Siofra there, but his eyes eventually adjusted to seeing them. They were beautiful. You could often tell one family from another by their clothes and the color they gave off. Bócrædere explained that the majority of fairy families are related most directly to the plants for which they care. "There are many stories for how this came about," he said to Alfred. "Some humans seem to have thought they are the spirits of the trees and plants themselves, dryads they often called them, or so Oliver Cyning told me. It is, however, very unlikely. There is nothing very wooden about them." Bócrædere was right. Their movements were just like those of humans, dwarves and elves, only much smaller, and winged. Alfred watched them clean the outside of the mound, he could only assume there was a large assembly of them cleansing the inside as well.

Siofra finally came out of the mound, but it was only to request the presence of Carlyle and Lucinda. "The Queen would like to see you," she said to them.

"Of course," replied Carlyle. "It would be our honour." The two of them entered the mound.

More time passed, night was coming on. Alfred and Bócrædere were sharing stories of the constellations as the stars began to appear. Hamorson sharpened and cleaned his weapons. Adelbert continued to finger his axe uneasily. Finally, Carlyle emerged from the mound. "Come friends, we will camp with the fairies this night. Our enemy is too long gone and night has now come, we will be at the disadvantage. But do not fret. We now have the fairies on our side. They will keep track of the goblins movements while we sleep so we may catch them tomorrow."

Adelbert was physically shaking as they entered the mound, still expecting some trick, but it never came. The cave looked different to Alfred now that the fairies had cleansed it. They had even made seats and tables of varying heights to accommodate humans and elves, dwarves, and fairies. At the very back of the cave stood Lucinda, deep in conversation, but they could not see with whom, at first. As Lucinda turned to greet them, however, they again felt they had been struck blind, by a light even brighter than Siofra's. As their sight began to return to them they heard a voice.

"Welcome, honoured guests. I am Queen Titania Elderflower. It has been long since the fairies have played host to such diverse and noble peoples. You are most welcome." She turned her gaze upon Adelbert. "Come Master Dwarf, there is no reason to fear. My fairies shall do you no mischief. You must remember that your stories of fairies are often as misguided as some of ours about dwarves. Why we once knew a story of a dwarf who loved gold so much he became a dragon. No more than you will become a dragon this evening shall we tie your beard in knots, pluck it out, or give you fey food that will make all others seem tasteless."

"O-of course, y-your majesty," said Adelbert. When he finally looked on her, he thought her more beautiful than any other creature or mineral he had ever seen. He bowed so deeply he fell over. The queen did not laugh, and silence those who did. She merely smiled at Adelbert.

"Your majesty," he said recollecting himself, "I have worked in the mines searching out the most beautiful gems and stones to work into beautiful artefacts. Yet the brightest gem pales in comparison to your beauty and light."

"You are most welcome here, Master Dwarf, as will all dwarves be if they have discovered your method of gilding their tongues." She laughed beautifully. "Come friends, join me as we drink to the health and peace of the forest." Each of them was brought a glass of wine and they drank deeply. Music and much celebration followed. The fairies are a generally happy people, sometimes naively so. The music Alfred heard was not like any he had heard before. It was as different from the music of the elves and dwarves as they were from each other. It had more of the earth and trees and flowers in it. It incited one to dance and laughter.

At the end of the festivities the fairy queen flew up to Alfred. "Dear Seer," she said to him, "come walk with me." In an instant she was standing beside Alfred, just as tall as he was and stunningly beautiful. Her hair was golden with streaks of silver, not grey, but silver as sterling. Alfred walked with her out of the mouth of the fairy mound. "What may I do for you, your majesty?" he said humbly.

"I need you to deliver a message for me. Tell the Faërie Queen that you are ready."

"Ready for what, your majesty?"

"You will see when the time comes. Can you do this for me, Seer?"

"I promise to try. I cannot say for certain when I shall see her, but as soon as I do, I will tell her."

"Excellent. Now, I think perhaps we should all sleep before my people make your dwarves over merry. Fairy wine is quite strong, even for dwarves. Tomorrow I will see you off. I have sent messages to all the fairy families that you and yours are to be helped on your quest. We fairies have perhaps been too dormant. We have not taken interest in the affairs of dwarves and elves, let alone the mortals, for centuries. Yet I feel the forest awakening at your coming. Or perhaps it is the goblins. It is too early to tell whether it is good or evil to which the forest awakes, but I will help you and the side of good. We cannot remain isolated forever."

The queen led him back into the mound, becoming small once again as she did so. The tables and chairs were gone and there were beds laid out for fairies, dwarves, elves, and Alfred. They prepared themselves for sleep and each slept soundly. Alfred thought of trying to have a vision again, but his mind was weary and he could focus on nothing. He drifted to sleep and remembered nothing until morning.

"Come friend, awake," Alfred heard the voice of Carlyle calling to him. "You sleep over long, my friend, though it is hard work when one has lengthy conversation with the fairy queen." He laughed and Alfred got himself out of bed. There was a basin of water set at the end of his so Alfred washed his face and hair, girded himself and sat down to a breakfast provided for the company. They saw neither light nor wing of a fairy that morning, but there were supplied laid out for them.

As they stepped out of the fairy mound there was the queen, big again, waiting for them. "Long has it been," she said, "since the fairies have had much to do with elves, dwarves, and men. Long has it been since we took an active role in the history of Elfland beyond guarding the forest. Today that changes. Today the fairies chose to work with the denizens of Elfland and against the evil of the goblins and their ilk.

"I do not have gifts to give my fellow citizens of Elfland, other than my friendship. To the Seer, however, I give a gift as a sign of my friendship with him and the fairies with humanity." She stepped toward Alfred carrying a necklace with a white gem on it. She fixed it around his neck.

"Now, with the faith and help of the fairies go in search of Oliver Cyning, stop the plot of the goblins. I send with you Siofra, to help and guide you when she can." Siofra flew toward them. The company made a bow to the fairy queen. Queen Titania bowed back, returned to her small size and flew off in the company of her fairies.

"Right," said Siofra. "Let's crack on, then."

Chapter 11

The seven of them went north, deeper into the forest. "This is the direction my cousins say they went," said Siofra as she led the way. Alfred watched her darting back and forth. She was keeping an eye out, both for signs in the vegetation that the goblins and trolls had gone by—they could not keep from damaging the forest as they walked through it—and looking for any other citizens of Elfland who might be able to tell them where they had gone. Days went by like this. Occasionally they would meet another fairy, once even a gnome, who pointed them in the right direction. Then they would speak briefly with Lucinda and Carlyle. Alfred wondered why the elves made sure to have a private conversation with each creature, but said nothing. Alfred continued to try to have visions at night, but to no avail.

They were now deep in heart of the forest. It was much darker, even cooler here than in the glades where he saw the elves, the dwarves' mountain, or even the fairy mound. "We must be getting closer to where they are gathering," said Bócrædere. "All our legends say that when the dark things in Elfland gather they suck the warmth and light out of a place."

"Tis true, friend dwarf," said Carlyle. "Yet they have not a full hold on this place. See! There are still places where the sun shines through." Carlyle was right. They looked and in a patch of sunlight grew a few wildflowers. They did not have time to admire them, however, for as they were looking on Alfred fell suddenly, as if something grabbed at his ankles. The others looked on in shock as a goblin, reddened and blistered from sneaking through the patches of sunlight, attacked Alfred, attempting to drag him off.

While stunned by the surprise, Alfred quickly grabbed up his sword and slashed at the goblin. It let go of him to avoid the sword and pulled out a wicked, twisted dagger of its own. The two battled, but the goblin was weary from its time in the sunlight. The fight lasted no more than a few minutes. The goblin's only hope had been in surprise. It collapsed in exhaustion at Alfred's feet.

"Go ahead human," it spat, "do your worst my people will avenge me."

Alfred raised his sword high above him, but brought it down next to the goblin. "I will not kill you, goblin, not like this." Hamorson objected.

"Kill that cursed nihtgengan, Master Seer. Or, if you have not the stomach to dispatch it, I will."

"No!" said Alfred, lifting his sword. "No one will harm this creature. I pity it. I pity anything that burns so much in even thin sunlight. Perhaps if we can introduce it slowly to things good and beautiful we can heal it. Bócrædere, have you ever heard tales of hobgoblins."

"Only a few bits and pieces have I found in our many stories concern hobgoblins. It is said they can live in the sunlight, that they love growing things, that they are only mischievous, not evil like goblins," Bócrædere replied.

"Oh don't listen to those old dwegorlingas' tales, Master Seer," replied Adelbert. "Let us kill it and be done."

"No. In a vision I saw two goblins walking, wondering if the hobgoblins would join them. They were in doubt. I wonder if we could cure this creature. Nothing is altogether evil, nothing is evil from the beginning. Perhaps we can work good on this pitiable creature." Alfred turned to look at the goblin when he felt a searing pain across the back of his leg. The goblin grabbed a knife and grazed Alfred's calf. There was little damage done. Alfred kicked the knife away from the goblin and asked for rope. Lucinda finally brought him some.

"You are wise, Seer, beyond your years. Good begets good," she said handing him the rope.

"I pray you are right, my Lady." Alfred tied the goblin's hands and gave it some water. They debated what to do with it now. The dwarves voted for tying it to a tree in direct sunlight; Siofra suggested playing some tricks on it to teach it fun rather than harm; Alfred rejected all these. "No, we shall teach it first to love fire for its light and warmth rather than destruction. We will rest here awhile and begin again in the evening."

Alfred tried to feed the goblin, asked it its name, but it refused food and conversation. He kept it in the shade and with Lucinda's help tended to its wounds. She then tended to his own. "You are lucky," she said wiping the dried blood from his calf. "The cut is not deep and the blade was not poisoned."

"No, indeed. Right glad I am. I have had my fill of goblin poison," he said thinking of his battle with the goblin in the tunnels. "This blade doesn't look like goblin-make. Is it elvish, Lady?"

Lucinda took the blade and passed it to Carlyle. "Nay," Carlyle replied "it is too rough for elf craft. It does not seem dwarven either. Hamorson?"

Hamorson took the blade and pronounced neither dwarven, elven, nor human. "The goblin must have made it. It is rough, but it has an elegance, one often missing from goblin-make."

Alfred puzzled over this. The goblin created a knife not only functional, but with a degree of beauty. Perhaps he was right to spare its life. Still, the goblin said nothing and growled when any came near him.

Things went on like this for several days. The group moved a bit more slowly, but in the right direction. Alfred knew this both from the information Siofra gathered for them amongst the smaller inhabitants of Fey Forest as well as the trees and plants themselves, as well as from watching the goblin. It began to be more on the alert. However, Alfred noticed that it seemed conflicted, both frightened and excited by what it smelled.

One evening, Alfred brought the goblin near to the fire. "This is the purpose of fire, goblin," he told it. "To warm and protect, and even to cook food for sustenance, not for torture and destruction."

"Poor, ugly goblin," Siofra said to him. "Here, have some food." She flew a piece of bread to its mouth. To everyone's astonishment, the goblin opened its mouth and ate the bread. "That's a good goblin," Siofra said to him.

"Hogsnout," it mumbled.

"What was that?" Siofra asked.

"Name's Hogsnout, Hogsnout Longarms," it grumbled through bites of bread.

"Nice to meet you, Hogsnout. I'm Siofra Rowan." She thought for a moment. "Can you help us, Hogsnout? We need to find the human the other goblins took. Where did they take him?" As she asked, Lucinda brought the ointments to treat Hogsnout's skin. The sun-sores were subsiding and even his pupils had grown smaller, more accustomed to light.

"Take this blasted rope off me, feed me some meat, and I'll tell you." He growled as Lucinda neared him. "Hmph, sorry. Old habits."

"I'm afraid we cannot yet trust you yet, Hogsnout," Lucinda told him as she bathed his wounds. "Your old habits might resurface. You will need to be able to endure the sun before we can trust you."

Hogsnout thought. "Tomorrow," he said at last. "Tomorrow, march in the sun, and head north toward the lake. If I cannot make it in the sun, leave me bound to a tree. If it's a trap, kill me first. But honest to the Faërie Queen, there's a cave nearby, its where the other goblins have taken that human. You'll have a fight on your hands, and no mistake. If it's as I say tomorrow, I recommend you give me a blade. I'm a damn sight more useful in a fight than tied up." The goblin ate a bit more from Siofra's hands, thanked her and Lucinda, as well as Alfred for sparing his life and went to sleep. Alfred tied the other end of the rope to a nearby tree and joined the others who gathered near the fire.

"We cannot trust it, I tell you," whispered Adelbert. "Kill it now like the vermin it is."

"I do not wish to kill it unworthily, but I still think it will betray us," replied Hamorson.

"Whether it does or no it would be wrong to kill it in its slumber. It is unawares, unarmed, helpless. We have fed and healed it. It is under our protection now. We may have to bring it to judgment for past deeds, but to kill it now would be worse than anything it has done," Carlyle finished and looked to Alfred. "Shall we trust Hogsnout, Seer?"

"If my sight is more than visions in the night, then I say yes. Its heart is good, or at least it wants to be. We will leave at first light tomorrow and follow the path he leads."

Adelbert grumbled, Bócrædere took notes, Hamorson prepared his weapons and the elves and the fairy tended to the fire. All went to sleep except Siofra who sat next to Hogsnout singing to him softly. She felt sorry for the poor ugly brute.

The night passed peacefully. Alfred had no visions, the sun was shining brightly and Hogsnout had done nothing wicked. They packed up their things, prepared themselves for battle and headed toward the lake. Alfred held the rope while Hogsnout led them, Siofra sitting on his shoulder. Lucinda and Carlyle followed after with the dwarves bringing up the rear. It was not long, however, before Adelbert made his way up to Alfred. He did not trust the goblin and if it were to try any mischief, he wanted to be nearby to stop it.

Hogsnout limped at first as they walked and squinted his eyes. His skin, however, did not crisp under the morning sun. Perhaps he was beginning to change, after all, thought Alfred. They walked slowly, Hogsnout sniffing out his way. He did not notice all the other fairies fleeing from him, nor the looks on their faces when they saw Siofra on his shoulder. What the trees and flowers themselves thought, I do not properly know.

Sniffing wildly, Hogsnout became panicked. "We're near now, he said, but they've got reinforcements. There's a giant nearby or I'm a gnome," he told Alfred. "They must have gotten one to guard the cave while the trolls and goblins sleep." Alfred was worried, he had once faced off against a giant with a whole troop of elves and come off much the worse for it. His chest winced with pain as he remembered that fight. They walked until they could just see the mouth of the cave and outside it, standing fifteen feet tall was a gruesome giant. Alfred could see Lucinda's face harden as she looked on the beast

"Once that giant defeated us, noble Seer, what say you? Shall we assail it?" Her face was hard as she looked at Alfred.

"I will not attack it unawares," Alfred said the dismay of the dwarves. "I will go forth and give them the opportunity to return Mr. Cyning to us without a battle. The goblins and trolls will not wish to fight us in the daylight and the giant may be made leery by our numbers and weapons. Hogsnout," he said turning to the goblin. "Is this the main camp of the goblins?"

"No," he replied. "That is back by the mountains. They were delivering the human to our king who is keeping himself on his throne on the other side of the forest"

"Good, then there will only be a few goblins and trolls at most, even if they have added to their numbers since I last had a vision."

Alfred steeled himself and stepped out into the clearing. The giant did not notice him at first, nor did he hear him. At last, Alfred picked up a rock and threw it at the giant's head. While doing it no harm, this drew the giant's attention.

"Giant!" Alfred shouted. "In that cave you hold a man. Release him or we will fight!" Alfred drew his sword and gave the giant a menacing look.

"Ho, ho, ho," laughed the giant. "The little man thinks he can hurt me. Take that!"

He swung his club at Alfred, but Alfred rolled out of the way just in time. He rolled towards the giant's legs and stabbed his sword into the giants foot! The giant howled in pain and began to stamp, trying to crush Alfred beneath his feet. Alfred, however, having breathed the air of Elfland for some time now, was nimbler than any human, and nearly as nimble as an elf. He stabbed the giant's foot again, but this time his sword became lodged in the foot.

Alfred was knocked back attempting to pull his sword from the giant's foot. The dwarves began to rush to him, but Carlyle and Lucinda stopped. "Give the boy a chance," they said calmly. Alfred pulled out the mattock King Hrothmor had given him. The giant swung its club at him, striking him in the shield. There was a loud clang. The shield rebuffed the giant's blow, but left Alfred shaken.

Alfred was heaving, out of breath. The giant also seemed slightly winded, but it could go much longer than Alfred could ever hope to. Alfred threw down his shield, and took his mattock in both hands. He swung first the pick at the giant's feet. It went home, but not as deeply as his sword. Then, Alfred had an idea. He turned the mattock and swung the hammer end as the giant swung its club. Just before the club connected with Alfred, the mattock struck the hilt of Alfred's sword, driving it deeper into the giant's foot.

The giant screamed in agony as blood poured forth from its foot. It attempted to lift its foot, but the sword now served as a nail, pinning the giant's foot the ground. The giant was surely strong enough to loose the sword, but the battle and blood loss made him weak.

"Yield giant," Alfred shouted as he staggered forward. He stumbled, but the elves and dwarves rushed forward to catch him. Before they could, however, Hogsnout reached Alfred and held him up.

"Yield to him, Rumbleweather," Hogsnout shouted to him. "It will go worse with you if you don't."

"Thank you, Hogsnout," Alfred said to him. "Come, giant. Come, Rumbleweather, yield and I will grant you your life. I do not desire your blood, merely the man kept in the cave and your departure. You may go and live in peace."

"Never," snarled the giant. Without any of them noticing, it grabbed its club and began to bring it down on Hogsnout and Alfred. Before it could reach them, however, the elves, dwarves, and even the fairy attacked the giant. His end was swift and club fell to the ground.

"Thank you, friends. You saved our lives," Alfred said to them. "Now, Lucinda, we are revenged on the giant, though I would have seen him yield."

"Your heart is pure, Seer," she said to Alfred. "I too do not glory in death, but death will continue to surround us while the goblins attempt to take the village."

"She's right, sire," Hogsnout said. "Come, let's get the human out of the cave, but be careful. The goblins and trolls are bound to have heard the battle, they will be waiting for us."

"Right you are, Hogsnout," Alfred said. "Adelbert," he said turning to the dwarf, "give our companion a weapon. He needs to be able to defend himself."

"You cannot be serious, Master Seer," Hamorson interjected before Adelbert could. "You don't mean to tell me you trust this, this nihtgengan?"

"I do. If he had wanted us dead, we'd be dead by now. Arm him, please."

Grudgingly, Adelbert handed Hogsnout a hammer, figuring he could do less damage with a blunt instrument. Hogsnout hefted it over his shoulder and the group walked into the cave, Alfred and Hogsnout at the lead.

They were quickly set upon by the goblins and trolls, but it was not much of a battle. Siofra tricked the trolls into going outside, where they were soon turned to stone. After that, most of the goblins, who were not killed, fled into the forest, screaming as the sun burned them and cursing Hogsnout as a traitor. None were injured, but while they checked each other over a voice from the back of the cave rang out. "Would someone be so kind as to undo these chains, please?"

"Mr. Cyning," Alfred exclaimed. They had nearly forgotten why they entered the cave in the first place, what with fighting a giant, trolls, and goblins. With the dwarves help, Mr. Cyning was loosed from his chains. Lucinda and Siofra looked to his wounds while Carlyle prepared some food for Mr. Cyning to eat. In fact, after inspection, the group decided to make camp in the cave. They were tired, it would be easy to defend themselves, and the goblins and trolls left behind many weapons and other oddments that might prove useful.

"Well, lad, you've certainly changed," Mr. Cyning said looking closely at Alfred. "You've taken to being a Seer. I can see it in your eyes. They see deeper now, don't they. Wait until you get back to the village, you'll see much deeper into things and no mistake."

"Lord Oliver," Carlyle broke in. "Have you learned anything from your time with enemy?"

"Only this, the Goblin King is on the move. They planned first on attacking the Queen, then moving in toward the village. After that, I believe they will try to take the mountain and the castle. We must prepare the people, elf, dwarf, hobgoblin, fairy, gnome, brownie. We'll wake the trees if we must, but the goblins must be stopped before they reach the village."

"They plan to attack the Fairy Queen?" Alfred asked, somewhat surprised. He knew she was strong, but strong enough to prove such an integral threat to their plans, surely not.

"No, Alfred. The Queen. The Queen of the forest. The Queen of Elfland. She often lives in a cottage by the lake."

"Not the old woman? She patched me up after my first bout with giant."

"Ah, yes. That would be her. She changes her appearance from time to time. Sometimes she's an old grandmotherly figure, sometimes a beautiful princess, sometimes even a hideous witch or ogress. She is the Queen of the whole of Elfland."

"Then why does she not reside in the castle?"

"That, my boy, is too complicated for right now. For now, we can trust she can take care of herself. We need to warn the dwarves, prepare the castle for siege and send a group to protect the village. First, however, we'll need to send out messengers to all the inhabitants of Elfland."

"The dwarves will be hard to convince to do anything more than tighten our security with my brother leading us," Hamorson said bitterly.

"Nevertheless, I recommend we send both Bócrædere and Adelbert to tell them what the goblins are planning."

"I'll get word to the fairies and the elves and the brownies and the gnomes," Siofra offered.

"Thank you, Siofra. Go quickly. We must wake the forest before our foes overcome us. Now then, what do we have here, a goblin?" Mr. Cyning looked over Hogsnout while the two dwarves and Siofra headed off. "A reformed goblin by the look of it, quite nearly a hobgoblin, I do believe. What is your name?"

"Hogsnout, my Lord," he mumbled.

"Let me look into your eyes, Hogsnout," Mr. Cyning grabbed hold of the goblin's shoulders, firmly, but gently. Then he stared, he stared long and hard into the goblin's large green eyes. At first Hogsnout fidgeted, but then he went a bit rigid, then limp, then he fainted. Still Mr. Cyning held him and studied him. "He will need to visit his cousins. Only they can finish the work you've begun, Alfred. Yes, I can read it in his eyes, you began the transformation. Only they can help him finish it. I will take him to the hobgoblins and then take myself to the castle to prepare."

"No," Alfred exclaimed. "We've only just rescued you! I'm not letting you go off alone."

"I let myself get captured, it was the only way to learn their plan. They certainly weren't going to kill me until they had delivered me to the Goblin King. Besides, lad, I won't be alone. I'll be taking Carlyle with me. We will go to the elves at court. You and Lucinda will go to prepare the defence of Carlisle."

And so the group that Alfred set out from the mountain with was reduced to himself, Hamorson, and Lucinda. Alfred was still at a loss for having just recovered Mr. Cyning and now watching him walk off with a goblin. Alfred trusted them both, though he could not say for certain why. A thought dawned him, as he, the elf, and the dwarf began the march back to Carlisle. "Why do you call him Lord Oliver?" he asked Lucinda and Hamorson.

"Why, lad, don't you know who he is?"

"He's Mr. Cyning, the storyteller in Carlisle, and if I had to guess, a seer."

"There is more concerning Lord Oliver than you know, Alfred, though you are right that he, like you, is a seer," Lucinda said solemnly.

"Has he ever told you any stories about the King of Elfland?"

"No," Alfred replied.

"The King of Elfland has never been one of our own people. Elfland is reminded of its connection to the mortal world by always being given a mortal to rule over it, usually a mortal man."

"Why a mortal man?"

"Because our Queen is an elf. I am of her line, her daughter, in fact, but she has not always been Queen. She is sister to the one who was King before her and he the son of the previous Queen. While we elves do not live so a frail a life as you humans, we can be cut down. This has happened several times in our history. Each time the closest kin whether descendent, sibling, or cousin and whether male or female takes the throne. They are always given a human partner to rule alongside them. Lord Oliver is our king, just as Lady Beatrice, my mother, is our Queen."

"Wait," said Alfred comprehension dawning on him. "Does that mean Mr. Cyning is your father?"

At this, Hamorson began to laugh so hard, a deep dwarvish laugh, that fell to the ground, gasping for air. Lucinda smiled at Alfred. "No, Master Seer. Elfland is not like your own country. Our monarchs are not married.

My Father, who was killed in the last battle with goblins, was not king, but was husband and consort to the queen, and an elf."

The three of them continued to walk. Hamorson was still giggling to himself, Lucinda smiled and began to sing, and Alfred walked as one dazed. He still had so many questions, but it seemed the time for questions was over for now. He had to steel himself for the mission ahead. He had to prepare his mind for the defence of Carlisle. He hoped Balthazar had reached his parents. He hoped they were preparing themselves as best they could. He began to wonder what it would look like, walking into the village with a dwarf and an elf, dressed for battle.

While he thought, Alfred could not help but notice the fairies in the trees and other small creatures he through might be brownies. They were clearly preparing themselves for something. The fairies were arming themselves with long thorns and the wingless creatures were putting armour made from what looked like nutshells. Alfred was so busy noticing the life of the forest that he did not notice the Lucinda and Hamorson had stopped and were now kneeling.

"How is your chest, dear Seer?" said the most beautiful voice Alfred had ever heard.

Chapter 12

Before the trio stood the most beautiful woman Alfred had ever seen. He had believed Lucinda was the most beautiful, but now, seeing the woman standing before him, Alfred felt as though he should avert his eyes. He felt as though somehow even his eyes were not worthy to look on such beauty. In the glances he allowed himself to steal, he noticed the woman was plainly dressed, a white dress was all she wore. Her feet were unshod and her neck unadorned. Round her head, however, was perched a wreath of holly. "I ask you again, how is your chest, dear Seer?" Alfred heard her say again.

"Fine, my lady, but how did you know my chest had been wounded?" he replied.

She smiled as she looked at him and answered, "Did I not tend to you myself? Do I not know the ones whom I have endeavoured to heal?"

"Lady?" Alfred asked. He looked behind her for the first time and noticed that she stood on the threshold of a small cottage. "I am confused. An old woman healed me when I first encountered the giant. She lived in a cottage by the lake. You, lady, possess all of her warmth but are more beautiful than any other I have ever seen."

"She and I are the same, dear Seer. I appear sometimes as an old woman, sometimes as a witch and sometimes as you see me now. And how do you fare my daughter, and you Prince Hamorson?"

It dawned on Alfred all of a sudden, this was the Elf Queen, Lucinda's mother. It was she who healed him of his first wound. Lucinda and Hamorson each bowed and responded to the lady while Alfred had his revelation. He caught her voice saying to all of them, "Come in my weary travellers and rest. You have much to do and must be rested."

They entered her cottage and Alfred found it just as it had been when she cared for him as an old woman. Hamorson, who was royalty in his own right and in a modestly dressed forest in the cottage, felt himself too low for the occasion. He begged leave to wait outside, fearing to dirty her home. "Nonsense," the Queen replied. "I am the Queen and may take whomever I choose into my home be they ever so dirty. Come, I will wash your faces and hands. You have seen many battles but few baths. Daughter, help me care for our visitors." Lucinda went into another room and when she and her mother returned, Hamorson was almost blinded by the radiance of the Elf Queen and her daughter, the Princess as he now realized.

The two of them helped Alfred and Hamorson take off their armour and outer clothes and washed their hands and faces and hair. The queen herself lovingly unknit the dwarf's beard, plaiting it again after washing it. "This is water from my lake, before the goblins despoiled it," the Queen told them. "It will rejuvenate you and wash away the weary you have experienced."

The Queen did not lie. Alfred and Hamorson felt not only clean but refreshed. They felt as if they had been given new life. Hamorson felt it perhaps more than Alfred for he had lived far longer. When the women finished, they washed each other and then the four of them sat down to a meal at the table. It was a simple meal: bread and honey, some fruit, nuts, and cold meats, and wine in abundance. Soon Alfred and Hamorson were singing and everyone was dancing.

After the meal Lucinda and Beatrice led Alfred and Hamorson to their room. In it were two beds. The ladies bade them good night. Seeing her now, Alfred saw Lucinda in a new light. She had become common to him, but now, with her mother, in this cottage, she was more beautiful than ever before, but older also, and lighter, and more serious, and younger. She laughed easily, but he saw clearly the weary in her eyes. He thought on this as he went to sleep.

"Blast," shouted a voice. A room full of goblins appeared around Alfred. They all trembled before a throne. "How could you have let the King escape?"

"They attacked in the daylight, sire. Their human defeated our giant. He is a terror to behold. Also, they had one of our own with them. It was Hogsnout. He has betrayed us—" The goblin stopped speaking suddenly as a dagger appeared sticking out of his chest.

"Send a messenger to our ally in the mountain. Tell him we make our move tomorrow, both in the mountain and on the village. If what my scouts tell me is true the castle is too well protected and the Queen's cottage has not been found. Still, perhaps if we conquer the mountain and village we will not need to worry about the King and Queen. We will be able to go out more directly into the human world and wipe that scum from the earth." The goblins cheered and Alfred's vision shifted into a dream.

When Alfred awoke the next morning he was troubled. There was someone helping the goblins from inside the mountain. But who? There were hundreds of dwarves in the mountain, it could be any of them. He dressed himself, but said nothing to Hamorson. I will wait until we are with the Queen and her daughter before I say anything, he thought to himself.

He went out into the dining room and found the table laid out for breakfast. There was more of the same kind of food they had had for dinner, but now milk and eggs replaced the wine and meat from their dinner. Alfred set to and was soon joined by the elf-ladies and Hamorson. "What have you seen, Alfred?" the Queen asked him.

"It is true, your majesty," he replied, "I have had a vision." He proceeded to tell them all he had seen and heard.

"It can't be," said Hamorson. "No dwarf would align himself with those, those nihtgengan."

"I can hardly believe it myself, Hamorson. I can only tell you what I heard. Perhaps the goblin king has some other kind of ally in the mountain."

"Perhaps," the Queen said slowly. "Nevertheless, I think it would be best if Hamorson were to return to the mountain. Do all you can to find out what is happening there. Send word by the fairies, they can always find me. Then draw together as many dwarves as you can and bring them to the edge of the forest by the village. I fear a large battle may still be in our future."

"Does that mean Alfred and I are to go alone to the village, Mother?" Lucinda asked.

"No, my dear daughter. I need your help with my preparations. My power alone will not suffice. Alfred must return and prepare the town as best he can."

"Your majesty," Alfred interjected, "no one will believe me. A few weeks ago and I would not have believed me."

"You must do your best. I will send to you to let you know where we have gathered. Join us once you have secured the village. I will also send word to the King and your husband, Lucinda. They should know what is going on and send as many as they can to help us in the battle. Come, there is no more time, we must all be off."

The four of them finished eating and began packing. Lucinda came to Alfred in his room. Hamorson was already on his way back to the mountain. "I come to give a blessing from my Mother and I," she said to him. She held a bottle out in front of her. "In this bottle is wine from elven vineyards. It will cure minor ills and refresh all who drink of it. My mother and I have blessed it. It may be useful in the days to come. My mother also bids me to give you this." She handed him silver circlet with a gem on it. "Wear it and all will know you are an elf-friend. The good creatures in Elfland will endeavour to help you and the evil will know that you are to be feared."

Alfred stood in bashful silence. The new eyes with which he saw Lucinda, made him feel he would utter nonsense should he try to speak, that he might profess his love for her or that he might go mad from being too long in her presence.

"Do you have nothing to say to me old friend?" she said, looking kindly on him. The spell was broken. He could see her now, both for who she was and for the Lucinda he had fought and walked beside.

"I am sad to leave you, my friend. Thank you for these gifts, I will bear them proudly," he said at last. "Would you tell your mother the fairy queen's message for me."

"She already knows," Lucinda replied, "that is why she is sending you home."

Lucinda walked forward and embraced Alfred. "My mother will not be able to see you off, but she wishes you well. She will send a message to you when we have gathered in the forest. I am afraid you are on your own from here. We will do what we can to protect Carlisle, but we must protect the forest as well. This is a difficult time when our enemy attacks on so many fronts." She placed the circlet on his brow and kissed him on the cheeks. "Go with the blessings of Elfland."

It was with a sad and heavy heart that Alfred once again left the Queen's cottage. How could he, just barely a man in the eyes of the villagers, convince them of the need to protect themselves? How could he make them believe in goblins? His parents would believe, but surely that would be it. Everyone else would think him mad or telling a bad joke. He walked through the forest. He wondered why Mr. Cyning never made things plainer for the people of Carlisle. Sure they would not have seen, as he is able to, but they could have been made to believe, some of them anyway. His parents did, many of the children did, or at least they wanted to.

"Perhaps this is how it is meant to be," Alfred said to himself. "Perhaps they aren't meant to know. Perhaps that is the Seer's job, telling them stories to keep the truth alive, but only enough to make them wish it be real, not enough to make it real. Few people would willingly live so close to danger. Even the good creatures, like the fairies, would play humans tricks, thinking it in good fun, that might hurt them."

Alfred pondered these thoughts as he soldiered on. At last he came to the edge of the forest. He could see the village, the church stood out in front from where he entered the village. He considered changing into his normal clothes until he realized he did not have any. His only clothing was elven. There was nothing for it but to walk boldly into the village and let people think what they might.

He stopped by the ancient church. It dawned on him that something should be done to keep the goblins from getting into the village from here. He stood outside staring off into the distance thinking about how he and his father might make their way down into the tunnel when he heard a voice calling to him. It was the voice of the vicar.

"Alfred, come in quick. You're parents are already here," the priest said to him quietly. The priest of St. Nicholas's Church in Carlisle was a bookish sort of man. His sermons were often well liked and full of references to stories Mr. Cyning told or other such fantastical works alongside Scripture and theologians past and present. He was neither a tall nor short man, of average weight, bearded, and there was a light in his eyes, an eternal kind of joy that was always ready to laugh. Alfred was surprised at the lack of surprise in the priest. "Fr. Stratford must not have noticed how I'm dressed, or the sword at my side," Alfred said to himself as he sauntered into the church.

"This way, this way," he said leading Alfred toward that portion of the church which held the secret passage to the mountain and the forest. Alfred thought nothing of this until he got closer. Not only were his parents in attendance, but there was Bócrædere, Siofra, and Balthazar. Alfred would have fainted with shock, but the elfish air he had soaked in over the past weeks would not be leaving his system any time soon and so he stood in shock, but in control of himself.

"What's going on here?" Alfred asked.

"So much to tell, Son, I'm not sure where to begin," his father said first

"Things are far worse than we could have imagined, Lad," Balthazar said to him. "The King has been captured, along with Carlyle and several of the King's court."

"The Queen too, and Lucinda have been taken, Alfred," Siofra piped in.

"What, how?" Alfred exclaimed.

"It's all our fault, Master Seer," sobbed Bócrædere.

"What do you mean, friend? What part have the dwarves played in this?"

"It was our king. He did not wish to save the dwarves, or he did but at a higher cost than any of us had expected. He was in league with the Goblin King. Apparently the Goblin King promised peace to Hrothmor in exchange for his help. He was to make it look like he was looking out purely for his own interests, which to his own mind he was, by not aiding you. Then, when the signal came he was to send out a small battalion of dwarves to aid in the fight against the humans and the King and Queen. It is because of the dwarves Hrothmor sent out, that the goblins had enough strength to take the King's castle and slew many within, taking captive the King and Carlyle."

"What about the Queen and Lucinda?" Alfred asked. "How were they taken? I thought them both far too strong."

"And so they would be, if they were not caught unawares, in the night by giants, trolls, and goblins," replied Balthazar.

"It's true," sobbed Siofra. "I saw it all, but I could do nothing. I tried to wake the trees, but I was not enough, my voice lacked command. They destroyed the Queen's cottage and took mother and daughter off I know not where." The tiny fairy drooped to Fr. Stratford's lap and sobbed uncontrollably.

"Alfred, we have to do something," his mother said, looking at him longingly.

"You're right. Bócrædere, how did you get out, and what about the other dwarves? Are there any who would join us?"

"We're forgetting one thing," said Fr. Stratford.

"What's that?" asked Alfred's father.

"They took the King and Queen and Lucinda and Carlyle captive. They didn't simply kill them. They'll be wanting something in return for their lives, though not their positions. If I had to guess, I'd say they want you, Alfred."

"Me? Why?" Alfred replied. "And where do you come in to all this anyway, Fr. Stratford? I thought this would be a bit outside your realm."

"A great man once said that God is the God of elves, and he was right. Remember that it was on his way to the Green Knight's chapel that a fairy castle appeared to Gawain just when he prayed for somewhere to celebrate Christmas. That being said, my story is too long. Suffice it to say that I knew Mr. Cyning when I was a lad.

"In this mess, there is one thing I can see quite clearly: The Goblin King wants to pull down the thrones of Elfland. He's made a deal with one, a deal he's sure to break, and has captured the other two and one of the heirs. They probably took Carlyle thinking he was the King's heir, and kept him when they discovered their mistake, knowing you'd want to rescue him. In the end, though, you'll be what they want. Even if they kill Beatrice, Lucinda, and Oliver, there will still be a king in Elfland."

Strong though his constitution was, Alfred nearly fainted at these words. King of Elfland? How could he be heir to that throne? He asked this very question. Balthazar answered:

"Since the first elves and humans formed societies there have always been royalty from each side on the throne of Elfland. It was a way to keep the peace. While the elven line usually runs through a family, the human is selected. Seers are rare, and it is always a Seer on the throne, they often remain unmarried. The few who have married and started families are not always blessed with children who can see. There have been stories about seventh sons of seventh sons being the only ones who can see, but this has never been verified.

"In any event, provided the current human King or Queen of Elfland has no progeny of their own, they look for children who can see in order to take over for them.

"When you moved here, Jessica and George, Lord Oliver saw something in you both. He knew you would do important things for both your own world and Elfland. He kept in touch, encouraged you to buy the Spoke when Mr. Bucklin was looking to sell, all to keep a close eye on you, and then you had Alfred.

"We all knew when once we saw you, my lad, that you would be Lord Oliver's heir. Elfland was all around you, wherever you went you took it with you. You saw us as well. A few of us were at your christening. My how you laughed when you saw us. And now you are needed. We must save the King and Queen and yet we cannot risk your life. If they capture you, they will kill you all, heirs and monarchs in one fell swoop. My wisdom is in knowing what has come before, but I cannot think of a time more dire than this." With that, Balthazar sat down and all were quiet.

All eyes were turned to Alfred. He knew now that this was his decision to make. He was the leader, not simply because he was a Seer, but because he was the heir, the prince. The weight of that thought at first seemed too much, as though he would not be able to bear it. Slowly, however, and even humbly, he realized, it had nothing to do with him. He was not special. The only traits he had that allowed him to do this were ones he had no choice over. The weight of his role in Elfland rested now comfortably on his shoulders. He knew what to do.

"Bócrædere," he said. "We need whatever dwarves are not on Hrothmor's side. Can you get together a group and have them meet us in the forest?"

"Me?" he replied trembling. "My Lord, I'm just a scribe. I am not a leader. We need Hamorson, or Adelbert. I cannot do this."

"You must," Alfred replied. "You are our only hope. You are the only one who can do this, but I will not send you alone.

"Siofra," he said turning to the fairy. She looked up at him, tears still streaming down her face. "I need you to go with Bócrædere. Give him courage and hope, for we have need of it."

The fairy dried her eyes, bowed, and said, "Y-yes, my Lord." She fluttered over to the dwarf and lighted on his shoulder. "Come, my friend," she said to him. "Let us be brave and do our Lord's bidding, for King Oliver, for Queen Beatrice, for Princess Lucinda, Lord Carlyle, and for all of Elfland." The fairy then kissed him on the cheek and the two of them bowed to Alfred.

"Find a way in, but know that we will be blocking the tunnel behind you. We cannot chance the goblins finding their way into Carlisle through the church," Alfred bade them farewell. Fr. Stratford said a prayer.

Alfred next turned to the gnome. "Balthazar," he said, "I know this is not the usual work of your people and if we had more dwarves I would ask them—"

"Say no more, my Lord. I will get my people together and we will cave in the tunnel. We may prefer the dirt, but enough moisture in the right place can always see mushrooms grow," Balthazar bowed low.

"Thank you, my parents, Fr. Stratford, and I will help you," Alfred heaved the mattock from his shoulder. "We must do this now, before we can do anything else."

Balthazar was sneaked outside and he swam away in the dirt. Meanwhile, George and Jessica raided their garden shed for anything that might help bring the tunnel down. Fr. Stratford was busy preparing the church, turning off lights, so no one would think it open, and locking the doors. Alfred ventured out to Mr. Cyning's cabin to look for any dwarfish tools that might be useful. They all returned within half an hour, Alfred bringing with him several pickaxes and his father and mother each carrying sledgehammers.

It was wearying, backbreaking work; and they constantly feared they would alert the dwarves, or any goblins still about in the tunnels and caves of the mountain, with all their racket. Still, they soon got enough rock down and had raised something like a wall in the tunnel that when Balthazar and the gnomes arrived, they had an easy enough job bringing enough stone and dirt down to block off the entrance to the church. It would be possible for dwarves or goblins to open up the tunnel again, but Fr. Stratford along with a few gnomes offered to stand guard and listen for tunnelling.

Despite all the time Alfred had already spent in Elfland, he still marvelled at the variety of gnomes. Some looked like Balthazar, large, overgrown chestnut mushrooms. Others, however, appeared like toadstools, morels, truffles, portobellos, and more. Alfred laughed to himself, despite the danger and urgency, over the abundance and variety of Elfland.

"The tunnel is blocked," said Balthazar, "and Fr. Stratford, as well as two other gnome chiefs, Caspar and Melchior, are standing guard with some of their people near the blockage. If anyone tries to tunnel through, we'll know about it.

"What do we do now, my Lord?"

Chapter 13

What do we do now? thought Alfred to himself. He sat quietly. "We have to rescue the King and Queen, but we mustn't leave Carlisle undefended," said Alfred at last

"Don't worry about that, my child," Jessica looked at her son, struck by both the weight now resting on his shoulders, as well as his ability to hold it. He had changed much and she saw it clearly. It made her both sad and proud. "We can defend the town, the three of us and the gnomes."

"That's right, son," said his father, "we'll take care of things here, you go do what you must"

"But my Lord," interjected Balthazar, "what if they capture you and kill you all, monarchs and heirs alike?"

"Then we shall die bravely and others will have to take our place," Alfred responded. "Do not worry, though, my friend. I intend to stay alive as long as I may. If we are going to rescue our friends we must do so during the day when most of them will be at their weakest, and who knows, help unlooked for may aid us. It certainly has thus far."

"How will you find them?" asked Balthazar.

"I will have to look for them in my dreams. In the meantime, let us prepare. Mum, Dad, Fr. Stratford, come with me to Mr. Cyning's cottage. There are a good many weapons stored there and stories concerning all manner of creatures, goblins, giants, trolls, and more. It would be good to read up on your enemies should they break through. Light and fire, however, are your best weapons."

With that the company prepared. Those who passed by the church remarked at the odd number of mushrooms which had creeped up around it. "Must be from the rains," mused one old man to another. No one had any inclination as to what it might truly mean. None of them was aware of the danger they were now in. All they noticed were some oddities, not least of which was Alfred in his elfish clothing.

"Must be getting ready for a medieval festival," said old Mrs. Edgar.

"He looks like a knight from one my stories," exclaimed an excitable little girl called Gabrielle. She also liked to stop by the church and stare at the mushrooms, though her mother could never understand why.

By the end of the day all their preparations were made. Alfred's parents, Fr. Stratford, and a host of gnomes took up residence in and around the church, preparing for an attack. Alfred, however, staid at Mr. Cyning's cottage. He read from the books he had taken, he searched through the other stories. He immersed himself in stories about goblins and giants and trolls and dragons and knights errant and princesses and elves and fairies and all manner of other such things.

Evening came on and Alfred was afraid. He was not afraid of battling the goblins, nor of death. Rather he was afraid of what might happen to his family, to his village, to the world should he fail. Above all, he was afraid he would have no dreams this night, or would not sleep at all. He laid himself down to sleep and before he had even fully closed his eyes a vision came to him.

Alfred's vision began in a cave. On the ground slept goblins, hundreds of them. Alfred looked to see if he could the mouth of the cave in order to determine where in the forest it was. What he saw instead horrified him. Strewn about the ground were dead fairies. Some of them had even been chewed on and others crushed after they were dead by what seemed enormous feet. He continued to survey the cave until he came upon what was clearly the Goblin King, seated on his throne.

This was Alfred's first opportunity to see the Goblin King closely. On his head sat a crown made of bones and blackened metal. He looked strange to Alfred; he differed somewhat from his fellow goblins. Not simply in size, but in shape and color as well. Not black or green was he as the goblins often were, but grey in color. He had hair, as well, jet black; but his teeth were sharp like other goblins. His hands and feet were almost like claws and were large. Alfred briefly noticed a vague resemblance to Hogsnout. Alfred's attention was quickly turned from the Goblin King himself, for at the his feet knelt Mr. Cyning, Queen Beatrice, her daughter Lucinda, and Lucinda's husband, Carlyle. They were clearly wounded, though, Mr. Cyning, being human, was much the worse for wear. Still, they each wore a stern expression.

"So you will not tell me about the other heir," snarled the Goblin King. "It matters not. Either he will come to rescue you, or, if he be too cowardly, I will find him when we enter the village. Death will be his as most assuredly it will be yours." The goblins and trolls seated around the goblin king's throne cackled with wicked laughter. Some even began to move toward the prisoners as if to bring about their deaths in that moment, taking their lord's words for a command.

The Goblin King held up his hand to stay them. "Not yet, my loyal subjects. Not yet. Their deaths will come swiftly, but if this human is as powerful a seer as I surmise, these three will serve us better alive than dead, for alive he may still seek their rescue and in his haste fall into my hands. Dead and though grief might drive him, it might also cool and steel him to think before he leapt." The goblins sniggered as they retreated from the prisoners. They sat down before them pulling out their blades to sharpen them.

"On second thought," said the Goblin King, "perhaps I can have somewhat of both. Bring me the he-elf. He is not of royal lineage, I have no other use for him." The goblins brought Carlyle forward and the goblin king pulled out his blade. Twisted and curved it was, and black. "Shall I kill you now, Carlyle, guardian and namesake of the village I am about destroy? Will your death drive our little seer mad with grief and cause him to stumble?" With that the goblin king lifted his sword to strike.

Before Alfred could see what happened next, however, his vision shifted. He was in a tunnel, but it felt different, it looked different. He recognized it as one of the many halls in the Dwerromount. There was a light in a nearby room off to one side of the tunnel. Alfred looked in and saw that the light came not from any fire nor electric device, but was the light of a fairy. Indeed, it was the light of Siofra herself. She sat on the shoulder of Bócrædere giving off light to a small gathering of dwarves. Alfred could not hear them, but he saw both Adelbert and Hamorson amongst the dwarves assembled. It was clear that Bócrædere was telling them of the misfortune and trying to persuade them to join Alfred and the others. Whether or not he was successful, Alfred could not say for sure for the vision changed once again.

Alfred found himself now in the forest. The sun was shining, which if that struck Alfred as strange it did so only briefly. For something more strange than the sun struck his eyes. The trees in this portion of the forest were large and old. Each was fitted with a door and windows, yet the trees seemed to be living, not dead. Wherever he was, Alfred thought it quite clear that this was a peaceful realm in the forest. One of the doors burst open and Alfred received a shock. Standing before him was none other than Hogsnout. He looked different. A coldness left his eyes and was replaced by what Alfred would normally have called a warmth, but this warmth seethed with indignation.

Other doors began to open and Hogsnout was joined by other creatures. They were similar to goblins, some more so than others, but they were different. They dressed, for one thing, rather cunningly, more than the rude tatters Alfred first found Hogsnout wearing. Their clothes were colorful, but now they were putting something on over their clothes. Alfred recognized it as a kind of leather armour. Each was embossed with beautiful designs. Almost Celtic or Saxon, Alfred thought it, like and yet unlike to the designs of the dwarves.

Alfred at first thought Hogsnout angry at the hobgoblins, for so he thought them to be. Now, however, he saw that this was not so. Clearly they had received news of the goings on in the forest. Each was now collecting its weapon. Some chose thin rapiers, others short broadswords. Hogsnout led them out, presumably to where he thought or knew the goblins to be.

"Alfred! Alfred!" someone shouted from what seemed like a distance. With a start did Alfred sit up in his bed to see his parents, Fr. Stratford, and a new face before him.

"What are you doing here?" Alfred asked in surprise.

"Well, I like that. Didn't I sit with you and listen to all the same stories? I may not be as gifted as you or even the Father here, but I've still got eyes in my head and ears besides," she smiled at him as she him. It was Winifrid; Wini Alfred had called her when they were children. Alfred had not thought of her for some time.

"Your parents contacted me," she said finally relieving the bewildered look on Alfred's face. "We need all the sympathetic people we can get if we're going to save the village. Sadly, it's the children who would be most willing to believe and help. We often forget how to see as we grow older."

"Well I know it," said Alfred. "It happened to me." He looked around and noticed it was dark again. "What time is it?" he asked.

"Nearly nine in the evening," answered his mother. "That's why we came. We were worried the goblins had already gotten you. Then we found you asleep and you were so hard to wake. We feared something had happened to you."

"I was having visions. I have seen much. Carlyle, I fear, is dead. Lucinda, Beatrice, and Mr. Cyning all survive. The Goblin King wants them alive until he can capture me."

"Carlyle?" Wini asked.

"An elf-lord, and Lucinda's husband. Lucinda is heir to the throne as am I, she through her mother Beatrice the Queen and me through Mr. Cyning."

Wini turned to Mr. and Mrs. Perkins. "I know you said you had a lot to tell me, but this goes beyond anything I could have imagined." Joy, wonder, and fear commingled in her eyes.

"What hope have we now," she asked, "if this goblin king has the king and queen and one of their heirs?"

"Bócrædere, Siofra, and Hamorson have gotten a small group of dwarves. If they can find a way out we'll have them on our side. There are the elves if they have gathered as the Queen had desired. There are also the hobgoblins."

"Hobgoblins?" Fr. Stratford, George, Jessica, and Wini all said.

"Yes, good goblins, or at least that is what some are, others are a breed all their own. I had captured a goblin, Hogsnout, and it seems he's changed, he's become good again. Mr. Cyning said he was going to direct him to the hobgoblins, but I never knew if he had succeeded until now. They are preparing for battle. Now so must we."

Alfred took his parents, childhood friend, and the priest to a back room in the cottage. He gave them more weapons. He could see a sense of fear in their eyes. They were afraid; they had never been in battle before. He realized that this was still new to him as well. His time in Elfland had given him a sense of courage, as well as experience, that these others had never yet had. It made him sad that this was the interaction with Elfland they were all having for the first time. He wished they all had been introduced in a time of peace. He wished it for himself. He wished Mr. Cyning were there rather than in chains bowed down before this despicable Goblin King.

They stayed at the cottage that night. The next morning, equipped with various weapons, Alfred attempted to instruct them in their use. He did not have much time, he needed to leave as soon as possible to rescue Mr. Cyning and the others. Still, he taught them all he could about the use of swords and axes. As evening approached, they all walked back to the church.

Once inside they were greeted by Balthazar. "My Lord," he said to Alfred with a bow.

"Have the elves gathered, Balthazar? And what about the dwarves and Siofra? Have they found a way out of the mountain?" asked Alfred.

"I do not know about the dwarves, but the elves and fairies have gathered at the castle. I deemed that the likeliest place the Goblin King would send a message calling for you to give up yourself."

"Excellent. Thank you, Balthazar. You have done well." Alfred then turned to the others. "I must go. I will leave you here with the gnomes. I will also try to send others to your aid in case I fail or the goblins decide to attack here first"

"You're leaving?" exclaimed his mother and Wini.

"I must. Someone must lead the attack. We have to rescue the King and Queen of Elfland. I am the only one who can do it."

"Why?" asked Wini. "Why does it have to be you?"

"Not for anything special about me, I've learned that much. It simply must be me. It is often that way, even in our favourite stories. It has to be me because I am the one who must do this. It is my doom in the old sense of the word.

"I must be off. Be safe. Take care of each other. Protect the villagers. If I make it back, well, I'll certainly have plenty of stories to tell at the pub, won't I?" Alfred smiled and walked out of the church. Alfred's mother began to weep, but steeled herself. His father looked grim and began to look after his sword; Fr. Stratford prayed. Winifrid said she would be back shortly.

Fr. Stratford waited up for Winifrid, but eventually his eyes succumbed to sleep. In the morning he and the Perkinses awoke. At first they assumed Winifrid was somewhere nearby. However, as they looked around the church and asked some of the gnomes, no sign of her could be found. Eventually, one of the gnomes on guard outside surveyed the dirt around the front door of the church.

"Someone's been by here not above six hours ago," she said.

"Six hours, are you sure, Macrina?" Fr. Stratford asked her.

"Quite sure, Father. We gnomes know our soil and this has been disturbed by a human walking away from the church last night."

Macrina could track her no further, however, for the walker had turned to the street and gnomes know little of concrete. The two of them went in and told Alfred's parents. Everyone wondered what could have possessed Winifrid to leave like that. George thought she might have been scared. It was, after all, quite a lot to take in, and in just a few days. Fr. Stratford and Jessica were not so sure, however. They thought perhaps something else guided her, but what neither would say.

Chapter 14

Alfred had told the others he was headed to the castle to muster their forces and wait for the demands of the Goblin King; he had lied. Alfred knew, somehow, that he must make his way to wherever the Goblin King was hiding the Queen, King, and Princess. He had all but given up hope on finding Carlyle alive, but he was determined to avenge him, if at all possible. He had set out late and was now in a dense overgrowth of trees. The air was close and the rays of the stars and moon barely were able to penetrate the darkness. Alfred did not lose heart, but he thought perhaps a fire might aid him. At the least it would welcome friends and ward off goblins, if not trolls or giants.

He thus set about collecting as much dead wood as he could find. This made barely enough to start a fire, let alone one that would last him the night. He pulled out a small axe he had taken from the King's cottage. He checked its blade; it was razor sharp. He walked to a nearby tree with low hanging branches. He swung his arms back. Before he started the forward swing he felt the axe being lifted out of his hands from above.

"None of that, now, little master, if you don't mind," said a booming voice above him as the axe came out of his hands. "I won't have you harming any of my trees."

Alfred drew his sword quickly and turned round. Looking up Alfred saw a strange sight. Before him stood a creature he could not quite place. It was not nearly as tall as the giant he had faced. However, it was much larger than he was, at least twice his height. It had a beard tucked into the belt of its tunic, but was completely bald on top, or so it seemed to Alfred who could not quite see to the top.

"Do you offer challenge?" Alfred shouted. "If so, then know that this sword has already been a giant's bane and I will set it to you if I must."

The giant's eyes widened in a smile that was just discernible beneath his monstrous beard. "No little master," he said with a laugh, "I offer you no challenge. I just won't have you hacking down my trees. It's taken me years to cultivate them." The giant got out a large pair of garden sheers and began trimming the trees.

"With whom do you stand," shouted Alfred, "the King and Queen of Elfland or the Goblin King?"

"Oh I don't stand with the Goblin King," murmured the giant, his attention being paid to the trees. "No, no, I stand with the King and Queen, the right and proper Queen and King mind you, but I mostly keep to myself. Why you're the first wight I've seen in an age. Few visit me here in the heart of the forest. Some are scared of me, I imagine, most have forgotten me. Still, here I stay, doing my duty, guarding and grooming the trees." He was thoughtful for a moment. He put down his enormous shears and turned to look at Alfred. "And who might you be, little master?"

Alfred was weary. To declare himself outright might prove his ruin. Yet this giant, while much smaller in height, seemed much larger in stature than the giant he had twice battled. "Alfred is my name, and I've come to rescue the King and Queen from the clutches of the Goblin King."

"Well met, Alfred," replied the giant. "Brynmor is my name, guardian of the heart of the forest. Now, what is this you are saying about the King and Queen? I can assure that both are far too strong and wise to be captured by some goblin chieftain."

"So much I know," said Alfred. "Nonetheless, they are captured. Queen Beatrice and King Alfred have been captured along with Princess Lucinda and Lord Carlyle, whom I fear, is dead. I must find them soon, Brynmor, or they may all be dead and Elfland leaderless."

"How do you know?"

"Parts of it I have seen with my own eyes. I have done battle with many goblins already who hope, along with destroying the monarchs and heirs of Elfland, to make their way into the mortal world through the village of Carlisle. Some other parts have been told to me by the dwarves who remain faithful to King and Queen. Balthazar the gnome has also told me much. Other news I have gathered as best I could."

Brynmor stared Alfred his face going from grim to disbelief to understanding. "You've said less than you could, Lord, and good it is to be wary. I was wary of you myself. It has been so long since a human has come so far on his own. I thought perhaps, well, we will not go into that. We must keep you safe and see if we cannot determine where this Goblin King is keeping the King and Queen. No more will we say for now. Come, I will take you to my home."

Alfred was still leery of this giant. Still, he trusted more in himself and his mission than he would have a month ago. So he followed the giant. They walked through a glade of trees more beautiful than any Alfred had ever seen. Their leaves seemed to be in a perpetual autumnal state; red, gold, orange, yellow, and green, the leaves swayed in the gentle breeze. At the end of the glade was a large house. It looked as though a series of trees had been nudged and encouraged to grow so that the end result was this house. Instead of shingles or thatch, its roof was composed of tightly interlocked branches. It would have suited as a two-story house for someone like Alfred, but the door and windows made it clear it was one story.

"Welcome to my home. Coed-tŷ, the men who lived here long ago called it. I liked the name and kept it, though many of them are now gone. Come and I will refresh you," the giant walked into his home.

Alfred looked on in awe. He thought his time in Elfland had steeled him against surprises. He was finding this not to be true. He entered the house with his hand on the hilt of his sword. No attack came. Instead a booming voice called out, "Come in, and know me better, man"

The giant disappeared into a back room but soon returned. The main room of Coed-tŷ loomed large. The ceiling was at least twenty feet high and all the chairs and the table would have made Alfred look like a child in an adult's room. Brynmor had changed, he wore green firs edged with holly and ivy. "Come in," he said again, "and know me better, Lord.

"Long have I served the Elfland court, long before the Saxons, before Arthur even. I have always been a servant of both the King and Queen. Now, you say they are in trouble and here you are their heir, on the mortal side at least, and tell me that the elven-heir has been taken too, and my old friend Carlyle." His eyes sank, his face fell, but only for a moment. The light returned to his countenance, "Tell me, Lord, what shall we do? What is your plan?"

Alfred thought. What was his plan? He had not given much thought to the particulars. In truth, he was simply trusting on his luck, or whatever it was that showed him what he needed to see in the visions and seemed to guide him to the right places. At last he said, "I do not think we can risk battle before we've rescued the captives. The Goblin King may trust to his ability to kill me in battle and simply execute the others. If I am to die, I would rather die knowing I have not left Elfland without king or queen. No, we must rescue the others before we can join the elves, dwarves, fairies, and hobgoblins who are now gathering at the castle. I cannot live knowing they may be subject to torture and murder."

"Well said, my Lord," exclaimed Brynmor. "We shall rescue them, you and I. We shall tear those cobs to pieces; we shall die in the attempt if we win not!" He slammed his large fist down on the table. "But we're moving too fast We have no notion where they are being kept, do we?"

"I only know they are in a cave, but one that looks out on the world. I do not think they are in the dwarves' mountain. They are somewhere else."

"It sounds like we need you to have another vision," said an unexpected voice.

Both giant and man turned to look at the doorway. There the form of a woman was visible. "Winifrid?" Alfred said startled. "What— How— When—"

"I followed you," she said lackadaisically. "You didn't think I'd let you come alone, did you?"

"But the village—"

"Is in good hands and is well protected. I think you'll need me before the end, Alfred."

Alfred was surprised, but in his heart he was glad to see her. He felt lonely. He felt the weight of this mission on his shoulders. In her presence that weight was lightened. Alfred introduced Brynmor and Winifrid. The giant bowed and Winifrid curtsied.

Winifrid brought the sword with her Alfred had given her and so they spent a few hours before dinner that night training. She was strong, stronger than Alfred would have given her credit for in the old days, but his time with Lucinda and Beatrice had taught him many things.

Brynmor went out to collect a few things. When he returned he had sacks of nuts as well as fresh fruit and honey. He also came with clothes and a shield for Winifrid. "The dress is the battle dress of the she-elves," he told her. "The shield belongs to Elfland Court." Emblazoned on it was a large Oak tree in white on a field of red and green. Brynmor went into his home to prepare dinner while Alfred continued to teach Winifrid about fighting. The Elfland air seemed to be working on Winifrid as it had on Alfred, she became stronger the longer they fought. At last Brynmor called them in for dinner.

There was bread and honey, nuts—roasted, salted, and raw, there were cooked fruit pies and raw fruit. They feasted and drank deeply from the large cups Brynmor provided them. The drink was like meed, but there was something more to it, something enlivening. After the meal Brynmor prepared beds for them. Alfred went to his bed exhausted but pleased. He needed to focus his attention on the King and Queen and Lucinda in order to ensure he had his vision.

Alfred tossed and turned for many hours, but at last he fell asleep and slipped into a vision. He returned to the cave he had seen before where the goblin king was holding his prisoners. The sun was gone down and so the goblins and trolls were quite active. Alfred could not see Mr. Cyning nor Beatrice nor Lucinda. But he moved closer to the mouth of the cave. It was rather small, probably intended to block as much sunlight as possible during the day.

Alfred could not understand just what these evil creatures were up to, but it seemed clear that they had been digging. To what end he could not discover. The goblins were working in silence. This alone Alfred found odd. What is more, he thought he could hear the sound of water running. They must be near the river, he thought to himself. Alfred noticed several oak trees which the goblins had felled. The vision faded and Alfred resumed his sleep.

When he woke the next morning, he told Brynmor all he had seen. "There are many deep hills and mounds by the river and the Queen's Lake," Brynmor said. "But if there are oak trees nearby they must be further north, close to the mountain range. It will take us several days to get there."

"Then we had better get going," said Winifrid.

"Wini," said Alfred, "I think you should go back to the village. Tell my parents and the others what we're planning."

"When are you going to get it through your thick skull that I'm not leaving you?" she replied. "You're going to need me before the end, I just know it. So stop trying to convince me to go home. I'm sticking by you."

"Alright. Then let's pack up and head out. Will you still come with us, Brynmor? We could certainly use your help."

"That I will, my Lord," Brynmor replied. "I think you will need me before the end as well."

It was settled. The three of them would head Northeast. Brynmor was almost certain that the trees Alfred had seen, and therefore the cave, would be on the same side of the river as the castle. Though he admitted that it had been an age since he had been so far. Alfred decided they would go as quickly and quietly as they could. This was a rescue mission, not a full assault on the Goblin King's forces. So they sneaked by the castle and even passed by the place where Alfred had once been in the Elf Queen's cottage. The place was familiar but the cottage was not there.

The three of them rested on its spot for the night. They had a feeling that it would protect them even if the cottage was gone. Part way through the night Alfred awoke. He had no visions, but something caused him to wake. Their fire had burned low, so he tended to it. In the light of the fire he could see the massive form of Brynmor laying next to him. He looked to see Winifrid, but she was not there. Her blanket and pack were where she had been sleeping, but she was not.

Alfred got up, realising how foolish it was not to set up a watch, no matter how safe they might feel on the spot where he had once stayed with the Elf Queen. His keen sight showed him that Winifrid had gotten up and walked towards the lake. He followed her footsteps and saw a pile of clothes laid out by the edge of the lake.

He strained his eyes and ears for any sign of her. The minutes that passed felt like hours as fear increasingly crept upon him. He was on the verge of shouting for her when he heard a splash in the lake. "Winifrid?" he called in a loud whisper.

"Alfred?" returned another loud whisper.

"Winifrid, where are you?"

"I'm coming, turn around."

"What? Why?"

"Just turn around, please."

It dawned on Alfred why this might be necessary and so he turned around. "Where have you been?" he asked with his back to her as she dressed.

"Let's go up to the fire first so I can dry off and get warm." She touched his shoulder and the two of them walked back to the fire. Winifrid sat down first and Alfred noticed she had something with her, a sword, but her own was still by her pack.

"Winifrid," he asked, "where did you get that?"

"That's what I have to tell you," she replied. "I had a hard time falling asleep. I was worried about who or what might find us in the middle of the night. I kept tossing and turning, trying to sleep, when suddenly I thought I heard something splashing in the lake. I went to see what it was, though I stupidly forgot my sword. Or maybe not. I could tell, somehow, that there was no danger, whatever the splashing was.

"I walked right up to the edge of the lake and there I saw a beautiful woman. 'Daughter,' she called out to me, 'come and join me. I have something to give you and something for you to give the Prince.' I trusted her implicitly. So, I disrobed, not wanting to have soaking wet clothes and waded out to her. The lake became deep rather quickly and soon I was swimming out to her. Each time I thought I was nearing her, she appeared just a little further away. Eventually, I saw her on land and so swam to its edge. I don't think it was any of the sides of the lake, it seemed more like an island.

"As I walked onto the shore she was standing there with a robe held out for me. I put it on and then she led me further in. There were trees everywhere at first, but then we walked into a little clearing with a stone pathway and what looked like old stone arches, but covered in ivy. The woman was standing in the middle by an old apple tree.

"'Come closer, my daughter,' she said to me. 'I am Nimuë, long have I lived between Elfland and the mortal world helping in the fight against those dark forces who raise their heads from time to time.' Then she gestured to a stone table behind her, by the tree. 'Here are two gifts, one I give to you and one I bid you give to Alfred.'

"I walked to the table. On it was this sword, which was for you. She told me, 'This sword has aided in many battles and has had many names. I will not tell you of its lineage tonight, though you and Alfred may learn of it hereafter.' After I took the gifts she walked me to the edge of the island. 'Go with my blessing, my daughter. I doubt very much I will see you again. With you and Alfred rest the hopes of your people, and mine.' Then she kissed me, like a mother, took my robe and I waded back out into the water."

"What about your gift?" Alfred asked.

Winifrid shifted her eyes downward. "That is a secret. She told me to keep it to myself for now."

Alfred knit his brow and began to think. The story sounded so familiar to him, but he glanced up for just a moment and looked at the sword and all other thoughts were swept from his mind. The sword was beautiful. It was expertly crafted and what few gems lay upon it gave it no opulence, but enhanced the beauty of its design. On one side of the sword were written these words, *tollite me*; on the other, *misit me*. Strange words to put on a sword, Alfred thought.

Winifrid and Alfred said no more to one another. Each was to lost in their own thoughts. Eventually both slipped into sleep and did not wake until Brynmor stirred the next morning. "Rise and shine, you two. Come on, don't we have some people to save?" Alfred and Winifrid both got up, but slowly. "You two look like you've had little sleep. Why don't you go splash some water on your faces? When you come back I'll have breakfast ready."

So the two of them walked down and said not a word to one another. They washed up and returned to the camp. "Now then, what happened at the Lake last night?" Brynmor asked.

"How did you—?" Alfred stammered.

"Come now, my Lord, I have ears as well as eyes. I heard you get up and I heard splashing in the Lake. Let's have it then, what happened?"

Alfred and Winifrid told their tales, haltingly and with many interruptions from one another, but none from Brynmor. When they finally finished, Brynmor asked to see the sword Alfred had been given. "This is truly a kingly gift, Alfred. Do you know who's sword this is?"

"Yes," Alfred replied. "It is Arthur's sword."

"Indeed, I've not seen it for an age upon an age. But it's more than that. This sword is far older than Arthur, this an ancient elvish blade, Alfred. Great harm may be inflicted with it, wars waged and won. But in peace and defence is where its true power lies."

"So I gathered from the writing, but what does it all mean?"

"Don't be quick to draw it, certainly never in anger. That was Arthur's mistake. When he used it to help the poor and oppressed and defend his lands things prospered, but when it became a tool of offence, well, you know the story."

"So it's all true, Arthur, Morgan le Fay, the Lady in the Lake?" asked Winifrid.

"Yes and no," Brynmor replied. "Not every story you hear is true and half the true stories have not be written. But you've met the Lady, Winifrid. Vivian, Evianne, Nimuë, she's had more names than I have. If we have her help and her blessing, I think we must go and rescue the others as soon as possible. Come, we must pack up and get to the Goblin King's cave before sunset. We won't stand a chance otherwise."

They packed up their camp and headed Northwest, Brynmor was certain this was the direction to the goblin king's cave. They walked for hours. Brynmor would occasionally sing softly to himself, words they could not understand, but the music reminded Alfred of the songs of the elves, but different, not as old, but more like the land it seemed to him.

There were many hills and caves as they continued to walk. In the distance further to the West, Alfred could see the Dwerromount. He wondered how Bócrædere and Hamorson were doing, and little Siofra. He wondered if the elves of the castle had gathered with them and if the hobgoblins had shown up yet. His thoughts turned back to the village as well, the gnomes, his parents, Fr. Stratford, were they safe, had any goblins attacked?

The day wore on and night was swiftly approaching. Brynmor had stopped singing and was walking even more quickly now. This made things difficult for Alfred and Winifrid who were nearly half his height. Suddenly, the giant stopped. Both Alfred and Winifrid looked to see what had made Brynmor stop. Then they saw it. Right in front of them was the river.

Chapter 15

They could hardly believe their misfortune. Brynmor had been so certain that they would be avoiding the river if they kept to the north side of the lake. "I just can't understand it," Brynmor said exasperated. "This is not how I remember it."

"How long has it been since you last came out this way, Brynmor?" Winifrid asked him.

Brynmor thought for a moment, "Seven, no, eight hundred years ago."

"The river must have meandered since then," said Winifrid.

"This world changes so quickly."

"Well, come," interjected Alfred, "we must decide what to do. I do not think going back and coming up the correct side of the river will do us any good. Who knows what the Goblin King might do in his haste. We will have to brave the river."

Winifrid and Brynmor agreed. The giant offered to carry them across. This seemed to make the most sense. They guessed the river could not be deeper than five feet, thus Brynmor should have no problem taking them and himself through the river. Brynmor hoisted the two humans on to his shoulders and waded out into the water.

The current pushed hard against him, but Brynmor was made of stern stuff, he belonged to this land and so the river was like a friend to him. He could feel its movements and plot his own accordingly. What they could not plan for, however, was a sudden drop in the middle of the river. The water was now up to the giant's shoulders and splashed about his face. It became difficult for him to continue walking.

"Brynmor, you will need to swim. We all will," Alfred told him.

Brynmor attempted to argue, but his mouth filled with water and he spluttered. So Winifrid and Alfred climbed off the giant's shoulders with their packs and began to swim toward shore. The day was waring on and the river was wide. They reached the shore and midday and the sun was now on its way down. Still, eventually, through much effort, the three of them finally made their way onto the shore as the sun was in its final hour.

"We must hurry," Alfred cried. "Soon the sun will be down the goblins will be able to give chase."

"Not to mention the trolls," Winifrid reminded him.

Drying off as quickly as they could and readying themselves for battle they walked towards the mouth of the cave. Quietly and slowly they made their way. Brynmor did all he could to be inconspicuous. He was surprisingly light of foot, as Alfred noticed. Still, they had to go as quickly as possible. Suddenly, however, Alfred stopped.

"What is it, Alfred?" Winifrid whispered. "We don't have time, the sun is setting."

Alfred knelt on the ground, however, next to a small group of mushrooms. He whispered to them, the others could not hear what he said, "Friend gnome, please spread the message, Alfred the Seer is attempting to rescue the King and Queen of Elfland as well as the Princess Lucinda. Tell any who are on our side to meet us here. We will battle the Goblin King here." The gnome did not speak, but suddenly the collection of mushrooms were gone. Alfred stood and continued forward.

He looked more determined than ever and neither Winifrid nor Brynmor asked him any questions. They reached the clearing in front of the cave. To their surprise, however, Alfred did not continue to sneak toward the cave. Instead he stepped out boldly into the fading sunlight. "Release your prisoners, Catseyes," said Alfred remembering what the goblins called their king. "Release them to me now and things may go well for you. Do not, and there will be a battle you cannot win." For a long while they heard nothing. Then laughter erupted from the cave. It was an evil laugh, full of malice and spite.

"You are just in time, whelp," said the voice belonging to the laugh. "The sun is setting and now that I have you, I can kill the king and queen and their heirs. I think I will begin with you!"

Goblins and trolls poured out of the cave. Alfred and the others could hardly believe how many there were. There seemed to be no end, until finally the last of them trickled out. Then, with laughter, out walked the goblin king. The moon shone brightly and Alfred could see the massive form of the Goblin King. He was nearly as big as a troll, but it was clear he was a goblin. His yellow, slanted eyes showed malice. His skin was grey and on his head he wore a black crown and his raiment was black. He was accompanied by three large trolls who dragged behind them the King and Queen and Lucinda.

"Come then," shouted Alfred. "Face me yourself, lord of the goblins!"

"Oh no, I am afraid my lineage is far too high to dirty my hands with blood so poor and so human as yours," said the Goblin King who believed goblinkind to be of greater nobility than humankind. "I have prepared a special death for you. It took me ages to find him, but the promise of roaming free and finding new hoards to gather as well as humans to kill was quite enticing. Was it not Isenmouthe?"

"Indeed, my lord," rasped a deep, booming voice.

Smoke billowed out of the mouth of the cave. Alfred readied his shield, but his sword he left in his its scabbard. A burst of fire shot out toward him, but his shield, being dwarven, protected him. If he had doubted what it was he was about to face, Alfred did so no longer.

The ground shook as the beast sauntered forth from the cave. It was a dragon, ancient and cruel. Its scales were like burnished bronze and stronger. Its wings flapped and cleared its smoke. The goblins and trolls formed a circle around the combatants. Several had taken Brynmor and Winifrid unawares, as they watched in terror. Alfred drew his sword. Again the drake breathed its fire on Alfred, and again his shield rebuffed it. Then it lunged.

Alfred side-stepped the dragon's attack. He went to bring his sword home on the dragon's neck, but the dragon moved swiftly. Still, his sword found its mark, if only just, and cut into the fat and sinew in the dragon's neck. Isenmouthe roared and his attack became more ferocious. Finding Alfred to be near his match on the ground, the dragon took to the skies. He tried again to breathe fire and so destroy his opponent. This was to no avail, as Alfred simply held his shield above him and so was protected.

Isenmouthe shifted tactics trying to bring its talons and teeth to home from above. Most glanced off Alfred's shield, but one attack, so glancing, found its way into his shield-arm's shoulder. Alfred cried out in pain as his shield fell from his hand and his arm hung lifeless at his side. The dragon saw this and brought himself down quickly on Alfred, talons outstretched. Alfred ducked the claws of the dragon, rolled, and as he came out of his roll thrust his sword upward. The dragon intended to crush Alfred beneath its weight and talons and so the combined force of Alfred's stab and its descent caused the sword to penetrate up to the hilt in the dragon's soft belly.

Screaming in agony the dragon belched forth fire, but the rent in its bowls caused the dragon too much pain and the fire was soon quenched. That the dragon was dead there was no doubt. Alfred's fate, however, had not been determined. The Goblin King had kept his head clear during the battle. He had already secured Winifrid and Brynmor between several trolls. Now he called the goblins and trolls to march. Winifrid, Brynmor, Beatrice, Mr. Cyning, and Lucinda were at the front of the group along with the Goblin King.

"Well, with that little nuisance dead or dying, I have not much need for the rest of you, not for long anyway. I wish for you to see me on your throne, with the village destroyed and then, with your hopes crushed, I will kill you," he said to the captives.

"Do you really think you can win?" Beatrice asked him. "Have the centuries taught you nothing? Has any of the evil you have committed brought you happiness?"

"Quiet! I do not desire happiness, I desire power, the right to rule, to have dominion, to destroy. I think I shall leave you alive when all is done. I desire you to see the destruction I am to bring to your precious world." Suddenly, as though he heard something, the Goblin King halted. "There's something out there." He turned to a small pack of goblins behind him, "You, go see what it is."

Before they had gone very far the twang of arrows could be heard. All around them, the captives saw goblins falling and trolls being enraged as most of the arrows bounced off them, but some found their marks. Soon the goblins and trolls were dispersing. The Goblin King himself had vanished from sight and the trolls to which they were chained were dead.

Out from the shadows came bodies much shorter than elves, though taller the gnomes. As they approached a casual observer might have assumed that is was the goblins returning. So Winifrid thought at first, but the monarchs and the princess next to her knew better.

"My Lord, my Ladies, are you all right?" asked a voice approaching from the shadows.

"A bit battered and bruised, perhaps, nothing that food, warmth, and disentanglement from these trolls won't be able to fix," answered Mr. Cyning. As the chains were undone he looked down. "Ah thank you, Hogsnout.

"I see you have managed to rally the hobgoblins."

"Indeed, my Lord, though they needed little rousing."

"It is true, sire," said another hobgoblin standing nearby. "We could feel it in our feet that something evil was afoot in the forest. When you brought Hogsnout to us and his rehabilitation was complete he began to tell us what he knew of the Goblin King's plots. Well, that had us enraged, but we were planning to meet up with the elves and the others closer to the mountain until we received the Prince's message. Where is the young Seer?"

"He-he fell," whispered Brynmor. "He battled the dragon and won, but in its death it crushed him."

Suddenly, realisation dawned on Winifrid's face. "I-I think I have something that can help him, but we must get to him quickly."

Unchained and with the hobgoblins and her fellow captives behind her, Winifrid began to run back to the glade where Alfred had fought the dragon. She ran up to the dragon and began to push with all her might. However, she was not nearly strong enough to move the beast's body. Brynmor soon joined her, but even he alone was not quite strong enough to move the dead the worm. It took the help of several hobgoblins before they were able to roll the dragon over. When they did, what they saw beneath it surprised them. Alfred was nowhere to be seen.

***

After the dragon came down upon him and the goblin king led his captives off, Alfred struggled to free himself and his sword from the beneath beast "Damn," he said exhausted after trying to shift the dragon off him. Straining again he realized he was not going anywhere. "My only hope is for someone to come looking for me, and with the goblins headed off with the king and queen of Elfland, that is unlikely."

"I would not say that," came a voice from next to him.

Alfred turned as much as he could and saw before him the unmistakable form of a gnome. "Ambrosius Puffball, at your service, he said with a sweeping bow and doffing his cap."

"Can you help me out from under this beast?" Alfred asked him.

"With a little help, my Lord, yes I can." The gnome then put his face down toward the ground, nearly right into it and gave a kind of call, a low note, almost as if from a hunting horn, but lower. Suddenly, it seemed to Alfred as though he was surrounded by mushrooms. Then, all at once, he felt a tugging. Slowly, as if through treacle, he found himself being pulled through the earth. The gnomes quickened their pace and before he knew it, Alfred was far away from the carcass of the dead dragon.

The gnomes helped Alfred hobble to a tree near the river's edge. Achingly, Alfred removed his clothes, torn, burnt, and covered in blood as they were, and went to wash in the river. Whatever enchantment was on the waters of the lake was clearly not as strong here, but the water still did him some good. He came back to shore and found that the gnomes had forgotten nothing and had grabbed his pack, weapons, and shield. He pulled out fresh clothes he had gotten from Brynmor, and dressed himself. He sat by the tree and began to munch on some of the food from his pack. Ambrosius swam up to him through the dirt.

"Lord," he said with a bow, "what are your orders? What should we do now?"

Alfred thought for a moment. The most important thing was to find out what had happened to the others and to gather as many of the good denizens of Elfland as possible to both protect the city and reclaim the goblin king's captives, assuming he had not killed them already. "We must send out scouts and messengers," Alfred said at last "We need to find out what the Goblin King is doing, and what has happened to our friends. However, we must also make contact with the elves, hobgoblins, dwarves, fairies, and anyone else who will fight alongside us."

"Very good, my Lord. I will send out some of my people directly." With that, the little gnome bowed and Alfred was left to rest

Alfred now realized just how exhausted he was and began to sleep. In sleep he saw yet another vision. He was in the forest, not far, it seemed from the cave where the Goblin King had been hiding. He could see into the glade where he had battled the dragon. He strained his eyes and saw his compatriots standing around the dragon. They were looking for him! Of course they were. He wondered how they escaped until he noticed small creatures, almost goblinish in size and appearance. The hobgoblins, he thought, must have rescued them. Alfred heard something in the forest behind him, it sounded like feet rushing quickly through the underbrush. Then the all too familiar twang of a bow echoed throughout the forest, he watched one of his friends fall, an arrow in their side. Alfred knew it was Mr. Cyning. He then tried as hard as he could to wake himself. Alfred woke and was furious.

Alfred pulled his sword from its scabbard and ran in the direction of the glade. He came upon a goblin unawares and slew it as he continued to rush toward his fallen mentor and king. A small skirmish was raging. There were only a few goblins and one troll. However, with the king wounded, the

Queen and Lucinda unarmed, and Brynmor fighting the troll, only Winifrid was able to do much fighting. She fought bravely and well. She was fighting three goblins at once, trying to keep them away from Mr. Cyning.

Alfred killed the goblins attempting to recapture the Queen and princess. He then turned to help Winifrid, but she had managed to fend off her attackers, Alfred's presence having frightened them. The troll also ran seeing he was alone and dawn was approaching. Alfred's lust for blood still pounded in his ears. It was several minutes before he remembered that Mr. Cyning was injured. He rushed to the old man's side.

"Alfred," Mr. Cyning said to him. "You're alive. We feared the worst." There was a catch in his breath. Alfred could tell it pained him to talk.

"Hush, Mr. Cyning," said Alfred, "don't talk. Rest. I'm sure Queen Beatrice can help you."

"Nay lad, my time is up, the wound is mortal. I must speak with you before I pass."

Alfred began to weep, "I will be lost without you, guide-less on this journey you have put me on."

"Me? No, lad, I have not put you on this journey. I merely discovered you were already on it. And you are not guide-less. You have the Queen, Lucinda, Carlyle, the dwarves, the fairies, the gnomes. You may be their ruler, but often will they serve to teach you a lesson. Remember my stories, tell them in the pub when this all over. Perhaps tell this one, just don't be too specific about the date." He sighed in pain.

"My time has come, lad. I'm proud of you. Be ruled first by love. It will not steer you wrong. Good-bye, son." With that, Mr. Cyning breathed his last

Alfred laid aside his sword, pulled out the arrow from Mr. Cyning's side and composed his body. Then he stood and shouted, "All hail the King of Elfland." The others gave a shout for King Oliver, Elf-friend. The gem on Alfred's brow began to glow. Alfred then collapsed to the ground and wept freely.

Having wept by his friend and mentor, Alfred called for a cairn to be raised, and quickly. He was now King of Elfland and he now had the full responsibility of protecting both it and the village. All looked to him to make a plan, even Queen Beatrice and her daughter, Lucinda.

"The Goblin King and his forces have been scattered by our worthy friends the hobgoblins," Alfred said standing before the old king's cairn. "Nevertheless, they will group. As the day wanes and the sun sinks they will gather themselves together for a fresh attack. They will surely try to reach the village tonight. Their plans have not come off and now they will have no time to lose. They will try to move swiftly while our forces are also scattered. In their haste is our hope.

"Gnomes! I call upon you, keepers of wisdom, to serve as messengers. I know speed is not your custom, but today we have need of it. Spread throughout the forest the call to defence. Ask all creatures to join with us in battle. Tell them to meet us at the glade by the base of the mountain. Warn them that they may find dwarves who are their foes and not their friends, but to be not swift in dealing out death. Go now!" The gnomes dove into the dirt as fish into water and went out.

"Hobgoblins! I thank you again for your aid. Join me now and march on the mountain. Perhaps we can turn the tide by causing the dwarves to choose between fighting with us or against us. Come, to the defence of both Elfland and the mortal world!" All those present shouted in affirmation. Then preparations to move out began.

"I still can't believe he's gone," said Winifrid in disbelief. "I've known Mr. Cyning my whole life. What will the world be like without him?"

"A little darker, for a while," said Beatrice. "But so is the lot of your people. One we elves have never fully understood. Yet now we must dry our tears and prepare. The world may be darker without King Oliver, but it will be darker still if the Goblin King gets his way."

"My Queen," said Alfred, "who is the Goblin King?"

"We do not often speak of it, for it is a part of our past of which we are not proud," she began solemnly. "Yet I think it will help for you to know more of our opponent.

"Before Alfred, before Arthur, before the Romans made landfall here in Logres, before even the Britons found their way here, the people of Elfland made this island their home. These faeries sought mastery over nature and made this island a paradise. Filling it with such variety as they loved, raising animals, crops, the land itself. How long they lived alone is unknown, but one day humans found their way to the island.

"At first the humans feared those they met, but slowly the faeries gained their trust and taught them many things. They taught them art of a new kind, that rolled like the hills. They taught them new music and ways of living and building. So things continued in peace and harmony, but in one amongst them hatred steadily grew.

"He was a hobgoblin and he hated the humans. He hated their ignorance, their inability to do so many things and yet their lack of reverence for we the long-lived. You see he wished them to see the faeries as gods, rulers over their fates, but his companions did not wish for this. So he bided his time, taking to him various creatures human and faerie alike, teaching them in private, secreting them away and telling none what happened to them.

"One day as the humans and faeries were working, they saw him come over the top of hill, at the head of a great army. Corrupted hobgoblins, giants, trolls, and other foul beasts followed in his train. The faeries held him off, aided by a group of humans; they were led by a woman, who it is said had descended from an elf mother and human father.

"When the battle was over, the Goblin King, as he now called himself, was banished from the sunlight, he and all those who followed him, by the King and Queen of Elfland. The King and Queen had been chosen that day, one the leader of the faeries and the other the leader of the humans. For the elves, the monarchy would pass through descendants, but for the humans, it was said that an estrangement would take place between men and elves and while all who would reign would come from the line of this woman, the descent would not always be direct. So, the history of our enemy is your history as well, King Alfred, and mine."

Finally it all began to make sense. Even the evil things in Elfland were not always so, they had been twisted by one who allowed hatred to enter his heart. Alfred pitied the Goblin King, but was resolved to stand against him.

"Thank you, my Queen," Alfred said to her, "Come, we must prepare to defend the village. Sound the horns, let the whole forest know that the King of Elfland goes to defend his realm. We will gather our forces on the border of the forest, by my predecessor's home. There is an open glade and much land before the village itself properly begins." Alfred had changed. He was no longer the listless young man who had entered the forest looking for mushrooms. Truly, as those who looked on him now had no doubt, was he the King of Elfland. The gem on his crown gleamed brighter.

And so they marched on. The hobgoblins blew their battle-horns and declared Alfred's intent. As they marched their numbers grew; fairies, gnomes, elves all joined in their train. The whole forest was alive and worked with the army of Elfland. As they marched on, they reached the summit of the mountain. Alfred called the army to a halt. "We must stop here, I would have words with my brothers of the mountain."

He walked in front of the army, Winifrid, Beatrice, Hogsnout, and Lucinda at his side, Brynmor looming behind them. "King Hrothmor, I call you forth to remember the oaths you made to King Oliver and Queen Beatrice. I, King Alfred, have need of your aid in the battle against the Goblin King to defend both the forest and the village. Will you join me?"

For a long while, there was silence. Then a voice could be heard replying, "The King of the dwarves awaits the King of Elfland. Bring with you a small party and he will greet you in his halls."

"Alfred," said Winifrid, "didn't you tell me that King Hrothmor had sided with the goblin king."

"Yes," replied Alfred.

"Well then you certainly cannot enter that mountain."

"I can and I will. Come with me, Winifrid, you also, Lucinda and Hogsnout. I'm afraid you are too large, Brynmor, and Queen Beatrice I would ask that you also remain behind."

"I prefer the trees to rocks anyway, my Lord," Brynmor replied.

"As you wish, dear King. My daughter will keep you safe," Beatrice replied.

The four them entered through a door that opened up in the side of the mountain. Immediately before them was a set of stairs. They saw no one as they climbed and they heard nothing. Only the flickering light of torches and the sound of their own footfall echoing engaged their senses as they climbed. If the others were afraid, they did not show it, they attached their will to Alfred's and climbed the stairs in silence.

When they reached the top they found a door. Before any could knock it opened quietly before them. At first there was no light, but slowly torches were lit. A few dwarves they saw, but none stayed to talk. The throne was in the distance before them. Alfred led the way.

"Well met, King Alfred. I am afraid your audience with King Hrothmor cannot be kept. He has been deposed. I now rule in his place. I hope I may serve you better than he would have."

"Indeed you can!" shouted Alfred with joy. "Hamorson!"

Lucinda also shouted for joy as she saw not only Hamorson, but Bócrædere, who's arm was in a sling, and Adelbert. Hogsnout remained wary, and Winifrid said nothing, for she had spent little time with Bócrædere and none with the rest of them.

"In truth, brother," said Alfred as he knelt to embrace the king, "while I came in confidence, I was uncertain of what I would find here. This least of all. How has it happened? Where is your brother? But be quick in the telling, we must soon march, if you have forces you can send."

"It is all thanks to Bócrædere, King Alfred," Hamorson replied. Bócrædere shuffled his feet and said nothing. "When he returned to us he rallied us. He told them of your plight and of that of the King and Queen of Elfland. Few at first desired to join him. My brother had done well to make the dwarves think their own protection of key importance. Nevertheless, he would not stop, reminding them of our stories of old and the valour of the dwarves. 'Are we naught but miners,' he said to them, 'or are we also warriors and defenders of the good?'

"Many began to rally to him in secret. He then had to find me, for only by putting another son of Hamor on the throne could he hope to bring the dwarves around. Adelbert and I had been locked up, deemed too dangerous to roam free within the mountain. Ha," Hamorson laughed, "my brother should have valued reading and scribes more highly, else he would have locked up Bócrædere as well and you would have naught to meet you but chains or death.

"Once freed, we began to meet in secret, spreading our message as quickly as possible. It was not long before we had rallied more than half the dwarves. Many only did my brother's bidding because he was king and not because they believed in his cause. Once gathered we took the throne room. There were skirmishes, and we did not come away unscathed though we came away victorious." It was now that Alfred noticed a long scar tracing down Hamorson's face and across one of his eyes which now stared out blindly. "The work of my brother," he said when he noticed Alfred staring.

"But come, we must prepare if we are to join you. Dwarves, arm yourselves, we go from battle to battle. We go to defend not only our mountain, but the forest and the world from the wickedness of the Goblin King and his forces!" With a shout the dwarves obeyed their new king and readied themselves for war.

Chapter 16

With the dwarves added to their company, Alfred led what must have been the strangest army ever seen. For not only were there humans and elves, and hobgoblins and dwarves, but the forest ground seemed alive with fungi as the gnomes walked alongside them. The air seemed to give off a light of its own as fairies joined their train. They reached the glade Alfred had been making for just before the edge of the forest Standing at the southernmost point of the glade, onlookers would have been able to see the old king's cottage.

Once they arrived, Alfred stood before his host and made an announcement. "Friends," he exclaimed, "today we ready ourselves for an assault, not simply on the village or on Elfland, but on what is good and beautiful and true. Because of this, ours must be a defence. Our enemy cannot understand defence, nor goodness, nor beauty. Only attack and sheer utility. For this reason, tonight we rest and feast, tomorrow, I will have a special need of the gnomes and fairies."

"Why not seek them out sire, take the battle to them?" asked King Hamorson.

"Because, my friend, they would be able to choose the ground on which to fight, and because I do not wish to tear up half the forest or the village in this battle," Alfred replied.

His companions throughout his journeys sat with him as they feasted that evening. Torches were lit in a large circle in elf fashion, but the music and food was dwarven. There was still some enmity between the hobgoblins and dwarves, however, until Hamorson and Adelbert approached Hogsnout.

"We've heard that you led the charge against the Goblin King's forces, that it is because of you our numbers are swelled with hobgoblins," said Hamorson.

"Yes," replied Hogsnout gruffly.

"Well done, lad!" boomed Hamorson, clapping him on the back. "We've been a bit stupid, I believe, Adelbert and I, concerning you. For that you have our apologies, and with our friendship you have our service." Both dwarves bowed lowly to Hogsnout.

"Come," said Adelbert, "let us drink together and you can tell us about the hobgoblins."

Hogsnout bowed in return and the three of them went off talking together. Their actions were a watershed as now all the hobgoblins and dwarves were mixing, drinking, feasting, and singing. Bócrædere could be seen, arm still in a sling, writing furiously in the midst of a group of hobgoblins, getting from them as many stories about themselves as he could.

Alfred looked out on the peoples before him, glad that the feast brought them together. He knew they would have no chance if the disparate peoples of Elfland could not be united in a seemingly smaller cause, food and drink. Alfred danced that night as never before. He danced with Lucinda and Beatrice, as well as Winifrid. Yet he also danced with the dwarf-women and hobgoblin-women who had accompanied them as well. At one point he saw Winifrid dancing with Hogsnout and smiled. Then he remembered what the morrow would bring.

While Alfred brooded there was a call for a story. Alfred called for Bócrædere, who was still furiously taking notes from some hobgoblins when the Queen's voice was heard. "Nay Lord," she said. "On this evening we should have a story from you, King Oliver was ever our storyteller and you have inherited his role."

So Alfred stood before his subjects, thinking only for a moment what story to tell and then began:

Once upon a time there was a terrible dragon called Isengrim. This dragon lived in the mountains of Britain and on occasion would fly down to the closest village to wreak havoc and steal treasure. Its own home, away in the mountains, was already filled to the brim with gold it had hoarded and stolen centuries earlier from a long forgotten kingdom. Many years had passed since the dragon had been seen in the village nearest the mountain, and the people began to think him only a legend. The dragon, however, was still quite alive, sleeping on top of its mountains of gold.

In the village there lived a boy, a young man not much beyond twenty winters. He was a good lad, always honest. He liked to make things and above all he liked to sing. He had a beautiful singing voice and could often be found wandering the streets of his village adorning them with his songs.

One day when the lad had naught else to do he began wandering over wilds surrounding the village. Whether it was a trick of his eyes or the will-o'-the-wisps, he thought he saw lights in the forest and began to follow them. Eventually he was led up the side of the mountain, though he did not at first notice it, as he was too busy singing. He began to wander off the path and still all the while singing:

> No jewel is so bright
> Nor can offer delight
> As the sound of my voice.
>
> All creatures would aid me
> And birds would trade me
> For this sound, if they had a choice.
>
> For no treasurer is greater,
> Nothing worth more,
> Than the sound of my voice.

Continually he sang as he walked and as he walked he sang until he found himself outside of a cave. Now Alfred, for that was the boy's name, knew better than to walk into an unknown cave. He had lived long enough to hear all the stories that could be remembered about Isengrim. Still, he thought to himself, it is unlikely that this is the wyrm's cave. So he stood in the entrance and began to sing again:

> The haunted hordes of dragons deep
> In the mountains where monsters sleep,
> Cannot kindle fear in one such as me.

"Oh really," replied a voice deep and unctuous. "Why not step inside to prove what you say."

"Nay, my lord. I could not trespass on your kindness, but if you would, why not come out into the sun with me for a stroll. It is such a fine day, and I could sing for you," Alfred replied.

Suddenly there was a rumbling within the cave and the ground beneath Alfred's feet shook when out sallied forth a large black and green dragon. It beats its wings and stretched its neck, not to be menacing, or not only so, but as if it had recently woken from a long slumber.

"Well met, Isengrim the Terrible," said Alfred with a bow. The dragon bowed in return.

"It seems man has not forgotten me, despite my slumber, but with whom do I have the pleasure of speaking?"

"Folk in the village call me silver-tongue and golden-lips. Some call me diamond voice. Others call me the friend of elves, while still others call me counselled by them."

"These cannot be your everyday names, they are far too long for common use."

"As for shorter names, boy, lad, you, but Singer is perhaps the most common, or Diamond. Either will do as it pleases you, O great Isengrim."

The dragon was still trying to puzzle out whether the boy was rich or not. He liked his voice, however, and thought to contrive to take the boy with the gilded-lips. "Well Diamond Singer, for so I shall call you, how would you like to live with me and sing for me always?"

Now, Alfred had no desire to stay with the dragon. He knew that one day the dragon would tire of him and eat him, or worse, as dragons can go much longer than other creatures without food or water, Alfred would die of starvation, singing to the great lizard. Still, a direct refusal was unwise, for it would anger the dragon.

"My lord, could anything be more desirable? Still, I must have some time to straighten my affairs and say my good-byes to friends and loved ones. May I have a week to prepare myself for your service?"

"An hour," replied the dragon.

"O lord, I am well loved for my voice, as I'm sure you can fathom as you value it so. I will need more than hour, why it would take me so long simply to reach the village. Give me five days, o calamitous one, I beg you."

"Hmph," snorted the dragon. "You may have one day, but should you not return, I will find you and burn your village to the ground and then eat you along with your friends and family."

"T'would only be fair. So we have a deal. I will return on the morrow at this hour to sing for you."

"See that you are on time. And tell no one why you are leaving. I do not fancy any knights discovering my home and trying their luck with me, though I am sure to conquer them." The dragon stood on his hindquarters. "As you can see the heat of my life melts the gold and silver of my bed and when they cool, they attach themselves to me so that I am armoured by scales above and precious metals below."

Alfred smiled and bowed and made many effusions concerning the strong and impenetrable armour of the dragon. All the while, however, his eyes were searching, for some kind chink, some missing scale, some place to wound the dragon. At last he saw it, there was a place above the beast's heart, or so Alfred presumed, where the gold and silver and jewels had not remained and the scales there were worn. Making his promise to return on the morrow and not to tell a soul what he was doing, Alfred bowed his way from the sight of the dragon.

As soon as the dragon had gone into his cave, Alfred turned around and ran down the mountainside as fast as he could. Perhaps the wisps had meant him mischief by leading him to the dragon's lair, but Alfred would make sure he benefited. You see, Alfred, who worked as an apprentice to the blacksmith, was descended from the earliest inhabitants of the village. In fact, many of his relatives had been killed and their gold stolen by Isengrim. He had once belonged to a rich and powerful family, though benevolent as well, but they were so no longer, not since the dragon.

Thus, when Alfred reached the village he begged his master to give him leave to work on a project for himself, and for the day off tomorrow as well. He promised he would repay him for the day's work and more besides.

"You need say nothing of paying me, lad," said the kindhearted blacksmith. "You work twice and oft' thrice as hard as any other apprentice I've had when you are here. Take the day off again tomorrow, and feel free to use the forge tonight. I for one am now for supper and bed."

"Good night and thank you, master," Alfred said as he stoked the fires. "You will not regret it."

With his master gone, Alfred got out the materials he needed and began to work on them, hammering and heating and cooling and heating and hammering. All the while he sang:

Strong be iron and strong be steel
Strong also arm and heart and will,
For dragon fire is hot and fierce,
And dragon hide be hard to pierce.

So he sang and hammered, but eventually, Alfred grew tired. He laid down his hammer and left his work unfinished. He thought to sleep but for a few minutes and resume his work, but slept soundly all through the night.

In the morning he woke in a terror, he had not finished and would have no time now before the dragon came in search of him. However, when went to look for them by the forge he saw them not. Where are my shield and my sword? he thought, but as he turned to the door he saw them there. Brownies had come during the night and brought with them a group of dwarves (brownies can do many things, but even they are aware that the skill of the dwarves far surpasses their own). There was a note attached. Alfred read it:

Go with the grace and blessings of all the peoples of Elfland. May these arms which you have begun and we have finished bring you to a good end. One warning we give you, however, offer the beast a chance to return what it has taken before you attack. Otherwise, the blessings we have placed on sword and shield will not protect you from the heat of the dragons.

Alfred praised his fortune that Faërie was with him and noted well the prohibition. He would need to steel his heart to walk up to the dragon's cave armed, but with sword undrawn.

And so he walked into the forest, finding again, though no wisps were present, that path that would lead him up to the dragon's cave. He sang no song, but felt an ineffable music welling up inside him as he climbed. Soon enough, or perhaps too soon, he arrived at the mouth of the dragon's lair. Alfred breathed.

"Come forth vile wyrm," he shouted with no hint of a quail in his voice as he drew his sword, "and redress the wrongs you have done to my family and my village."

A thundering sounded forth from inside the cave. Isengrim breathed smoke so that it obscured his exit from the cave. "What's this?" he growled. "Has my minstrel returned without a song, but with a sword and shield. Tsk tsk. I shall have to punish you for this." The dragon breathed fire.

While his sight was obscured, Alfred had the ears of a singer and knew from which direction the dragon's voice came. Thus, as it sought to incinerate him on the spot, he was ready with his shield. "You have stolen from my family," Alfred shouted. "You have stolen from and killed many in my village. Will you repay your wrongs? Do so and I shall leave you not destitute and with your life. Refuse and you will be left without wealth or life."

"You may have a strong shield, mortal, but you have seen my hide, no sword made by man can pierce even its weakest place."

"So you refuse my offer?"

"Yes," hissed the dragon and for a moment Alfred lost his sense of where the dragon was.

Then, it attacked, striking out with one of its claws. Alfred's shield protected him again. The dragon struck at him again, but this time Alfred sidestepped the blow and struck one of his own. It did not cut deep and drew no blood, but the force and sharpness of it was nevertheless felt, unexpectedly by the dragon. This bug had a sting that could annoy and possibly hurt.

And so the battle waged on. Neither side doing any real hurt to the other, though both beginning to tire. However, the old dragon had one last manoeuvre it had not yet employed. It feigned as if it were going to strike with its front claws. As Alfred jumped back, however, he found himself gathered in the beast's hind claws and lifted quite suddenly up into the air.

"Your shield may be strong," laughed the dragon, "but it will not protect from a fall, I think. How about I take you home, little minstrel, I can visit your village and add more gold to my stores and flesh to my belly."

Up, up it soared and in the distance Alfred could see his village. Once overhead, the dragon grabbed Alfred with its fore claws and said to him, "One last song for your master, minstrel?"

"Yes," Alfred replied, "a funeral march." And with that Alfred drove his sword into the weak point in the dragon's chest and pierced its enormous heart. Screaming in agony the dragon twisted in the air and began to plummet towards the earth.

With a crash it landed and the village was shaken as if by an earthquake. No one had been killed when the dragon fell, but much of the town was destroyed. The smith had seen the note Alfred had left behind that had been attached to his arms. Realising that the, as he then thought him, foolish boy might bring harm to the village, caused as many of them to flee to safety. They had only just left the centre of the village when the dragon came crashing down. The smith was the only one brave enough to approach the wyrm. He expected to find both boy and beast dead. Imagine, then, his surprise when he found Alfred, shield on his arm and sword, blackened by the drake's hot blood, in his hand rising from atop the beast

The smith shouted for joy and few of the other brave villagers ventured to what they thought would be his rescue only to discover the dragon dead and the boy alive. Soon the whole village was gathered 'round the dead beast singing and shouting. If anyone wondered how they would repair the village that was soon answered as Alfred told them where the dragon's cave was and that they could reclaim the wealth that had once belonged to them.

It took many trips to and from the dragon's den to bring all the gold and jewels to the village. Much of it was given to Alfred as both the slayer of the beast and belonging to the family from whom much of it was taken. The village was eventually rebuilt and the beast buried. Alfred was then known as Dragon's Bane and used much of his wealth to patronise the arts. He became something of a king in the region, though it was said in later years that he spent much of his time in the woods. Many believed him searching for those who gave him the tools to defeat the dragon. Others thought he had found them and went oft to learn wisdom from the folk of Faërie. When Alfred had lived long, much longer than is usual for a human, he died and though his kingdom is now long forgotten, still this tale is told of him, the tale of Alfred and the Dragon.

***

When Alfred finished there was silence at first, a long silence, then, applause. "Well done, King Alfred," said the Queen. "It has ever been the job of the human King or Queen of Elfland to tell stories, some true in one way, some true in others, about our realm. In this way it is protected from being forgotten, from falling into obscurity through lack of utility, as humans are wont to do."

"You mean I am meant to be a storyteller like King Oliver?" Alfred asked, surprised.

"Indeed. Many have devised different means of keeping our memory alive, some have told stories as you have done, others have written poetry or songs. In many ages past when one could be both King or Queen in Elfland as well as in the human world, they would often employ those more skilled at telling tales, usually others gifted with the sight. Taliesen was one such, instructed by both Arthur and Merlin. As time has passed, however, the crown has often fallen to those able to tell the stories themselves. But come, my liege, we must sleep. Tomorrow will soon be here."

Chapter 17

That morning battle preparations began. Alfred sent out scouts to try to discover the enemy's position. It was imperative that they drive them to the glade where Alfred and his army waited for them. Hogsnout led the scouts and when they returned, they were fairly certain they knew where the enemy was hiding.

"Well done, Hogsnout," Alfred said to him. "One thing more, I need you now to take a large group and begin planting torches, have the fairies and gnomes help you. We need them to form a blockade that will cause the enemy to come toward us. When evening begins have the fairies and gnomes ignite their torches, the fire should help drive the Goblin King to us."

"Yes, my lord," Hogsnout replied and ran to collect his scouts as well as gnomes and fairies.

It was a strange sight, thought Alfred. Here before him were fairies, gnomes, dwarves, hobgoblins, a giant, two elves, and two humans, including himself. The sight was so strange to him precisely because he did not find it strange. A month ago he would have laughed at the notion that any of these creatures were real, let alone that he would be their king about to lead them in battle. Off to one side he saw Lucinda and Winifrid. It looked like Lucinda had decided to continue the training Alfred had begun.

"I don't know what it is," said Winifrid, "but I feel stronger, faster. Not so much as you, but more so than I ever have been."

"It is the air of Elfland," Lucinda told her. "On mortals it can work only one of two effects, strength or fear." Winifrid received another attack from Lucinda and not only defended herself, but managed to disarm the elven princess. "Oh well done," cried Lucinda. "Yes, you will do well, you will fight bravely."

Alfred continued to walk through his troops. He saw Brynmor amongst the trees, even before a battle he could not help but tend to his flock. The dwarves and hobgoblins were working together, sharing weapons and armour. Most of the gnomes and fairies had gone, either they were with Hogsnout or back in the village. Alfred thought of his parents and the priest back at the church. If his plan worked they would not see any harm and would be safe. This comforted him.

As he continued to walk he began to miss Mr. Cyning sorely. Now especially could he use his guidance. The Queen and Princess were excellent counsellors, but he desired the counsel of a human and one older than himself. Every Arthur needs his Merlin, he thought to himself, but even Arthur did not have Merlin forever. "And look where that got him," he said aloud.

"Look at where what got whom?" Alfred turned around and saw Winifrid standing nearby him.

"No one," said Arthur. "I just miss Mr. Cyning. I feel like he would be able to tell me if what I'm doing is right or wrong. He would be able to guide me."

"Like a Merlin to your Arthur," said Winifrid. "I miss him too," she looked at Alfred and saw tears in his eyes.

"I'm sorry we haven't had more time to talk," Alfred said, falling somewhat back into his old self.

"Alfred," she said incredulously, "you've been preparing a defence, you've been preparing for war. I think you've had enough on your plate. Besides, I've been spending time with Lucinda and Beatrice, they've been teaching me to fight, though they say you did a decent job of getting me started. Still, I've a good dose of natural talent."

Alfred laughed, not at Winifrid, but just laughed at the insanity of it all. Here he was with his childhood friend discussing the death of a mentor, which would be normal, if it were not for the war preparations going on all around them, and those being carried out by dwarves and hobgoblins. Winifrid joined him in laughing and stood closer to him.

Alfred turned to look at Winifrid and finally the Seer's eyes were opened. "What did the Lady give you that night on Avalon?" he asked her.

"Oh," she was caught off guard by the question. "Well, as to that—" she was clearly flustered. Alfred moved towards her, but then the air rang out with horns from the forest. The sun was covered by clouds and night was beginning to arrive. Alfred tore himself away from Winifrid.

"To arms!" he shouted. "To arms! Night comes and our enemy has used the clouds to his advantage. To arms! Defend Elfland, defend Carlisle! We will stop them here."

There was a hustle and bustle as the dwarves and hobgoblins began to arrange themselves for battle. The forest floor in front of them seemed to be moving, but Alfred realized it was the gnomes. "The enemy is coming! They shouted. Our plan has succeeded, but they come much sooner than we had planned," they shouted. Alfred ran out to them and began quickly to talk with them. Soon, almost as one body, the gnomes began to dig into the soil far out in front of the army.

Hogsnout appeared with the last of the gnomes and fairies. He was wounded. Siofra was flitting around him, trying to care for his wounds. "Hold still you great lout," she spat at him, "or you'll bleed to death."

Still, he bowed before Alfred and spoke, "The enemy caught us unawares as we began to light the torches. I thought perhaps we should light them before dark to ensure their being ready in time. Still, I would never have imagined the goblins and trolls being willing to risk being caught in the sunlight should the clouds break. We lit the fires and enemy scouts were revealed. One gave me this," he pointed to a wound in his side, "but he did not find his way back to his master."

"Well done, Hogsnout," Alfred then turned and sought the Queen with his eyes. "Dear Queen, you once healed me of grievous wound, can you aid this wounded hobgoblin?"

"Indeed I can. Come with me my child," she said, turning to Hogsnout. Siofra continued to fuss over the hobgoblin as the three of them walked behind the lines of defence.

Suddenly the air was full of a violent noise. The air was rent with the sound of the goblin trumpets. Perhaps they would have attacked in secret, as is often their wont, but the torches were a surprise. In any event, the escape of the gnomes ensured that their enemy would be wise to their coming. So the Goblin King declared his presence. If he sought to intimidate, it had a mixed effect. The dwarves and hobgoblins were not intimated by the presence of their enemies, rather it was the numbers. There were two giants, a host of trolls and unnumbered goblins. Discounting the larger enemies, the dwarves and hobgoblins were easily outnumbered three-to-one. Still, they steeled themselves for a fight. Alfred was at their head and when they looked at him their fear grew less.

"Go back!" he shouted. "Your darkness cannot prevail, you will not reach the village, you will not spread to the mortal world and I will stop even your spread in Elfland if I may."

In answer, a goblin shot an arrow at Alfred which glanced off his shield. Alfred's own forces responded in kind. A volley of arrows was shot and much of the Goblin King's front line fell, dead or wounded. The rest were urged forwards for the battle to commence in earnest

Still Alfred's army waited, shooting the occasional volley of arrows, but not moving forward to engage their enemy. The goblins and trolls soon discovered why. Many were falling into the pits and trenches dug by the gnomes. Soon, however, the majority had crossed beyond the line of holes. The giants, with their long legs arrived first. Arrows were bouncing off them. Still Alfred did not draw his sword. One them lifted its club above its head to strike Alfred and those around him. In a swift motion, Alfred drew his sword and stabbed it into the giant's foot. The giant howled with pain and stumbled backwards, falling to the ground under the momentum of its swing. Then was Alfred's army unleashed.

Brynmor ran forward to fight with the other giant while the dwarves and hobgoblins closest to Alfred dispatched the one in front of them. Then Alfred and his army charged and the battle was commenced in earnest

Hamorson and Adelbert were fighting one of the trolls which kept trying to crush them with the large hammer it carried. The dwarves kept dodging the weapon and would retaliate with blows about its feet and legs. Then in a rage, the troll began swinging its hammer like a golf club and Hamorson was lifted off his feet.

In another fray were Lucinda and Winifrid battling a small host of goblins. The ladies were fighting bravely, but the more goblins they dispatched, the more there seemed to appear. Winifrid cried out in pain. She was wounded.

The Queen and most of the fairies stayed back from the battle. The Fairy Queen, however, would flit in and out of the battle bringing with her wounded warriors to be healed at the ministrations of Beatrice and the fairies. Soon they had more than they could help and most attempted to go back to the battle after being patched up.

Alfred himself was attempting to make his way to the Goblin King, but would stop to help those being overwhelmed around him. The Goblin King himself took no part in the battle, but sat at the rear of his troops watching.

It looked as though they would lose the battle when horns were once again heard in the forest Alfred's forces were at first dismayed, they believed it to be a signal to the Goblin King's forces that reinforcements had arrived. However, the goblins and trolls looked just as concerned. Then, without warning, bursting forth from the trees came an army of elves and at their head, Carlyle.

Alfred nearly sang with joy at the sight of Carlyle. Though he could not quite hear her, he was certain that Lucinda had. Carlyle and his elves fell to quickly and the tide began to turn.

As the fight wore on, however, neither side was gaining ground. Brynmor and the still living giant were locked in combat; the rest of Alfred's forces, however, were only able to keep the enemy from gaining ground. There was only one thing Alfred could think to do as the hours wore on.

Alfred fought his way through the battlefield until he reached the very edge of the enemy lines. Before him stood an enormous goblin. It was a foot taller than he was and had arms that nearly reached the ground. Behind it sat the Goblin King upon his throne. The goblin snarled and leaped at Alfred.

Alfred knocked aside its arms with his shield and smote it upon its head with the hilt of his sword. The great beast fell unconscious at his feet as he walked towards the Goblin King. "Coward," said Alfred. "Why do you sit here? Are you preparing to escape?

"I know what you are, Catseyes, a deranged hobgoblin of old. How do you feel knowing that a human is about to best your forces? You hated my people, did you not, for coming to this island and taking away from your greatness? What then will you do? Continue to hide upon your throne or will you give up now and repent of your ways? Only one option more will I give you, join the fight and do battle with me."

Alfred's words found their mark and with a snarl the Goblin King leapt from his seat, drawing at the same time his sword. Though he moved quickly, Alfred was prepared for the attack. The evil king's sword struck Alfred's shield and a tone rang out, long and loud. All the warriors ceased their fighting to see what was happening. Soon Alfred and the Goblin King were battling fiercely.

Alfred kept himself on the defensive at first, only deflecting the attacks of the Goblin King. This only served to enrage him. "Fight back!" he shouted as Alfred dodged another blow. Still, however, as the night wore on Alfred would only occasionally venture a blow, but his were less likely to miss. Still, it was not long before both combatants were bleeding freely.

Hours seemed to pass as the two of them remained locked in combat. The fighting around them began again, but a wide birth was given for the King of Elfland and the king of the goblins. Alfred thought to weary his opponent but his plan seemed to have backfired. Instead of growing more weary with the passage of time, King Catseyes appeared to become more ferocious. Still, though he was an ancient hobgoblin, the wounds Alfred dealt did begin to weary him, but not as quickly as Alfred was wearied.

It was not long before more of the Goblin King's blows found their marks. No matter how strong the Elfland air may have made Alfred, it was clear he was no match for this evil creature. Alfred went in for an attack and found his legs struck out from under him. The Goblin King laughed as Alfred struggled to rise. "Darkness will finally have its day and I will have my revenge," said the Goblin King as he raised his sword. Just as he began to bring it down screams of pain and agony erupted around them. Indeed, King Catseyes himself screamed and his blow went wide, though it still ran Alfred through. Alfred looked up in his own pain; the sun was shining.

All around the forest glade trolls were turning to stone and goblins were fleeing into the denser woods attempting to hide. Brynmor threw down his opponent and ran over to the trees and spoke to them. Soon the trees were letting in more light as the goblins tried to escape. Many were captured and several killed. There was much rejoicing until all looked to the place where Alfred and the Goblin King had been fighting.

As the sun shone and the evil king's sword came down, Alfred's own sword went up. Unlike the Goblin King, who pierced Alfred's side, the King of Elfland sent his blade true. Both were now bleeding freely lying upon the field, one dead, the other alive.

Alfred's companions from his journeys through Elfland gathered around him: Brynmor, Hogsnout, Lucinda, Adelbert, Hamorson, Siofra, Carlyle, only Beatrice and Winifrid were missing. "Where is the Queen," Alfred asked, "and Winifrid? I would speak with them." The others looked around for them while Siofra attempted to tend to his wound. At last they were found, and the Queen and the woman walked together arm in arm.

"It is time, child," Queen Beatrice said to Winifrid, "you are ready and so is he."

Alfred tried to speak, but tears welled up in his eyes as he looked at Winifrid. She was worn and tired and battered from the battle, but he found her radiant. Indeed, a light seemed to shine out from her as she drew near. "Don't speak," she said to him. Winifrid knelt beside Alfred and to the surprise of nearly all, placed her hands on the sword in Alfred's side and pulled it out. "This is what she gave me," she whispered in his ear. Then she placed one hand on Alfred's side, and, tears streaming down her face, she kissed him.

Then from her pocket she pulled out a flask and a cup. She poured water from the flask into the cup and poured it on Alfred's wound. The water poured out red. There was a bright light and the cup was gone, as was the wound in Alfred's side. "What happened?" asked Alfred as he sat up.

"The Lady of the Lake gave me a cup that would heal a mortal wound and water from the fountain of Avalon. She told me I would know when to use them," Winifrid replied.

"How did you know now was the right time?" Alfred asked.

Tears welled in Winifrid's eyes, "Because I would love the person dying so much that their death would be as my own."

Alfred, with tears streaming from his face as well embraced Winifrid and kissed her. Those around them began to cheer and laugh and soon every creature of Elfland that was present was laughing and cheering for their King was alive and they had won the battle.

Chapter 18

The fairies and Queens Beatrice and Titania were kept quite busy the rest of the day healing the wounded. Meanwhile, the dwarves, hobgoblins, and captured goblins were set to digging graves for those who had fallen. The dead were not too numerous and Alfred was thankful for that. With all the necessary tasks complete, Alfred assembled his army and his captives before him.

"My friends," he exclaimed, "today we have won the battle. Evil has been staved off once again." Cheers erupted from the host before him. "Still, we must keep vigilance. Evil may rise again. This time we saw it begin in our own people. Our brothers the dwarves have had to fight and slay their own. In order to keep the evil out of the forest we must first keep it out of our hearts! This is why we must tell this story, the story of the battle on the edge of Elfland. We must tell it to our children's children's children. This is my task in the village and the world beyond. For Elfland, I entrust the task to all of you, but I leave in charge of the telling of stories Master Bócrædere." Many cheers followed, particularly from the centre of a group of dwarves where Bócrædere was standing. "Come forward, my friend."

As the dwarf hobbled forward, still wounded, Alfred knelt in front of him. "Into your hands I commit the writing and telling of this story for all in Elfland. I want the whole forest alive with this story. Will you do that for me Master Storyteller."

"Yes, my Lord," said the dwarf with a bow.

"Now my friends, I must leave you. It is not right for humans, not even a King or Queen of Elfland, to always dwell here. It is our duty to remain in the mortal world and tell your stories so that we humans do not forget. I will come again soon for I have not had the honour of staying in the Castle. For now, however, I leave you in the hands of your Queen, Beatrice, her daughter Lucinda, Lucinda's husband Carlyle, King Hamorson, and the Master Storyteller." Alfred stepped down from the platform on which he was standing and took Winifrid's hands into his own. "It is time to go home," he said to her. "Are you ready?"

"As ready as I can be to face the mortal world again now that I know all this is here. I am sad to be leaving," she replied.

"You've seen too much for it to go anywhere. I promise you that," Alfred kissed her softly.

As the host was decamping, Alfred walked over to the hobgoblins and asked Hogsnout, who had become a leader amongst them, to watch over the goblins. Hogsnout promised to do so and Alfred promised to visit them soon. The good-byes were all said and none were left now save the Queen, Lucinda, Carlyle, and King Hamorson.

"Good-bye, fair elven folk. May your lands be little troubled in the years to come," Alfred said to them.

"Farewell, Seer and King of Elfland," returned Carlyle. "May we see you soon at the castle."

"I will come as soon as I can, I have many things to attend to in Carlisle. I am anxious to return."

"Fare thee well, my liege," said Queen Beatrice, "and farewell to you daughter and now sister to my daughter Lucinda, for so she views you. Come back to us as often as you may."

"My mountain is always open to you both," said Hamorson. "Perhaps in the future we can again open the tunnels and increase the connection between the village and the forest Who knows when we may have need of it." The dwarf bowed to Alfred and Alfred returned the bow.

He and Winifrid walked together out of the forest, past the old King's Cottage and into the village. Everyone in the village was staring at them and little should they have been surprised, they were holding hands for one which would have set all the village gossips to talking on its own. However, they were still clad in the raiment of the elves and this too caused heads to turn. Still, they walked on, in love but melancholic, or perhaps simply nostalgic for Elfland or something more. Perhaps Elfland itself awakened in them desires they never knew were there.

When they arrived at the church they were shocked. All about lay dead gnomes and goblins. Quickly, forgetting all else, they ran inside. Standing before them were Fr. Stratford, Alfred's mother Jessica, and Balthazar. Alfred's father was reclining on a pew nearby.

"It seems there are many stories here to tell," said Alfred. "But first I think it wise to dispose of the dead."

"Don't worry, my Lord," said Balthazar, "the gnomes will see to it." He walked outside and Alfred and Winifrid were left with the other humans.

It seems that during their battle in the forest, the Goblin King had sent a battalion of goblins into the village at night, hoping to distract the forces of Elfland and take the city. He had not counted on there being a resistance. Alfred's father was wounded and many of the gnomes were wounded and some dead, but they held off the attack until daylight which sent the goblins left alive running.

In the days that followed Alfred and Winifrid were married by Fr. Stratford in St. Nicholas's Church. They invited the whole town and while many were surprised, none were displeased with the service. "It had an air about it," said Millicent Caldecott. "It seemed both earthy and airy, if those are the right words." Others said it felt royal somehow and common, high and low. They all thought it was beautiful.

After the wedding Alfred and Winifrid moved into Mr. Cyning's cottage. The old man had left it to him in his will. There was a funeral for Oliver Cyning and many were in attendance, many seen as well as unseen.

The happy couple soon began a large flower garden as well as small farm on the land surrounding the cottage. Finer flowers, fruit, and vegetables could not be found anywhere, or so the locals said. People began to come from miles around just to view the gardens. Many called them enchanting or even magical.

Several years later when Alfred's parents passed, he took over The Broken Spoke as well. He would tell stories to enraptured patrons. Winifrid meanwhile spent most of her time in the gardens and in the forest, until one day it was announced that Alfred and Winifrid were expecting. They say she had a home birth, but some swore they saw her enter the forest and return with her baby. Whatever the case, the little girl born to them had a glint in her eyes, that always made people laugh deep joyful laughs when they saw her. She was called Lucinda Olivia Beatrice Perkins and a lordly looking couple no one in the village recognized were made her godparents at her baptism.

And so it was that I found them, the happy family sitting in their pub, telling stories, wandering around gardens and forests, drinking excellent beer, and eating excellent food. I had been drawn to this little village while I was a Ph.D. Candidate in England. I had heard stories, even in Nottingham, about this little village of Carlisle and a great storyteller who had lived there. There was a rumor he had died, but if he was still alive, I was bent on meeting him. I bid my wife farewell one morning, and made my way by train, bus, and foot to the village of Carlisle. I met the new owners of The Broken Spoke and asked them about the old storyteller. I will never forget the look Alfred gave me, as if he was sizing me up and pleased with what he saw. He told me that the man's name had been Oliver Cyning and that he had died several years ago. I was saddened at the news. "Come back this evening," said Alfred to me. "I may not be as good as Mr. Cyning, but I know all his stories and tell them myself in the evenings. Yes, come back tonight and you can hear a story and maybe we can speak more after."

As I sat in the pub that evening I heard Alfred tell the story about the naming of The Broken Spoke. I asked him if I could write it down. Alfred said I could, but first we went for a walk in the gardens which led to a walk in the forest. What precisely Alfred saw in me I still don't know, what I saw in the forest no one would ever believe. Still, after that venture, we returned to the pub and Alfred told me he had a better story for me to write, the story of how a boy named Alfred and a girl named Winifrid helped save the village of Carlisle and Elfland as well.